**With Spring's lovely blue eyes
gazing up at him so seriously,
Marco felt tongue-tied
like a young boy.**

Why hadn't the years toughened him so that
this beautiful, unattainable woman would no
longer have the power to make him want to
pull her close for a stolen kiss?

*Spring Kirkland—I thought I'd completely
forgotten you.* But his heart had played him
for a fool again. He still wanted her. He still
couldn't have her.

Books by Lyn Cote

Love Inspired

Never Alone #30
New Man in Town #66
Hope's Garden #111
Finally Home #137
Finally Found #162

LYN COTE

Born in Texas, raised in Illinois on the shore of Lake Michigan, Lyn now lives in Iowa with her real-life hero and their son and daughter—both teens. Lyn has spent her adult life as a teacher, then a full-time mom, now a writer.

When she married her hero over twenty years ago, she "married" the north woods of Wisconsin, too. Recently she and her husband bought a fixer-upper cabin on a lake there. Lyn spends most of each summer sitting by the lake, writing. As she writes, her Siamese cat, Shadow, likes to curl up on Lyn's lap to keep her company. By the way, Lyn's last name is pronounced "Coty."

Finally Found
Lyn Cote

Published by Steeple Hill Books™

STEEPLE HILL BOOKS

Steeple
Hill™

ISBN 0-373-87169-4

FINALLY FOUND

Copyright © 2002 by Lyn Cote

Visit us at www.steeplehill.com

Printed in U.S.A.

In all your ways acknowledge Him,
and He shall direct your paths.
—*Proverbs* 3:6

Dedication

Thanks to Roxanne Rustand,
my award-winning critique partner.
I'm honored to call you friend.
And to my sister, Carole.
Thanks for being a great sister.

Acknowledgments:

Thanks to Doris Rangel
for information of the *quinceañería*.
And special thanks to Priscilla Kissinger, aka
Priscilla Oilveras, for help with my fledgling Spanish.
¡Gracias!

Prologue

"God Rest Ye Merry, Gentlemen" played softly in the background. Everything around Spring Kirkland harmonized to create a holiday scene worthy of gracing any Christmas card. The windows of her parents' new home were fogged with moisture from the warmth from gingerbread baking in the kitchen. But nothing in this holiday setting distracted Spring from the hidden purpose for her trip home.

Her sister, Hannah, wearing a red-and-green apron, flipped on the oven light and leaned over, peering through the glass oven door. "These gingerbread cookies are just about golden around the edges." Without glancing over her shoulder, she added, "Doree, keep your fingers out of that frosting."

Pulling her finger back from where it had been poised over the bowl of white butter cream, Doree exclaimed, "You're no fun! I was only going to steal a taste."

Though Spring's nerves moved her to start pacing, her sisters' sparring amused her. Dark-haired Hannah, the professional cook and food writer, was in her element: the kitchen. Blond Doree, their younger sister, still in college, was enjoying her role as family tease.

The three of them had been left alone in their parents' brand-new house in Petite Portage, Wisconsin, to bake cookies for the Christmas Eve service at church in two days. Ever since Spring had arrived last night, one unspoken question had been hanging over them. With their parents out of the house, the time finally had come to ask *the question*. She cleared her throat.

The timer on the stove buzzed. Hannah set about lifting the sheets of cookies out of the oven. The fragrance of gingerbread filled the air.

Spring started again. "Hannah, you said you had some news for us about—"

Someone knocked on the door. Spring went to answer it. "Oh, hi, Guthrie." Holding in her frustration, she stepped back to let him in.

"Guthrie!" Hannah flew to the kitchen doorway, still holding the spatula in one hand and wearing a Christmas oven mitt on the other.

"Mmm." Guthrie made a sound of approval. "Sure smells good in here." He drew Hannah close for a quick hello kiss.

Hannah giggled and kissed him back.

Folding her arms in front of her, Spring felt torn. She couldn't help beaming at them. Hannah had certainly found her match in Guthrie Thomas, the carpenter who'd built her parents' home. But why did he have to stop by right now? They only had until their parents returned to discuss this!

"Guthrie, I'm amazed at the creative excuses you come up with to see Hannah." Doree smirked from the other end of the kitchen where she leaned against the doorjamb. "What explanation are you using this time?"

Guthrie chuckled. "No excuse. Just dropped in to greet your sister, Spring."

"Then, say hi to her," Doree instructed dryly with a motion of her hand. "You haven't even looked at her—"

"All in good time," Hannah murmured, then she moved aside to let Guthrie take a few steps forward.

Guthrie held out his hand to Spring.

She gripped it. "Oh, you're cold."

"Yeah, the temperature is dropping, all right. Glad you're here, Spring. Hope you enjoy your first Christmas in Petite."

"I'm sure I will."

She'd liked Guthrie, her sister's fiancé, from the very first time she'd met him, but she wanted to get to the topic topmost in her mind. She glanced at Doree and saw the same anxiousness reflected there.

Guthrie turned his attention back to Hannah. "I have to go do some chores at the farm, then I'll be back to take the three of you out to the tree farm to get your family tree."

Hannah kissed him lightly on the cheek. "Thanks.

I just have two more balls of dough to roll out and bake. We can finish frosting them afterward.''

Guthrie kissed her cheek, then left with a wave. Spring closed the door behind him, shivering in the cold draft.

"You two have got it bad," Doree taunted cheerfully.

Hannah smiled and walked toward the oven. "You can start frosting and decorating the first batch now. It should be cool enough."

Spring halted near them. If she didn't ask the question quick, someone else might interrupt. "Hannah, tell us what you found on Mother's birth certificate."

Hannah continued placing raw cut-out cookies one by one onto a baking sheet. "What I *didn't* find was what was really important."

"Then, what didn't you find?" Sitting at the table, Doree started frosting the first cookie.

"Mom's birth certificate had been altered to show only the adoptive, not the natural, parents." Hannah glanced up.

"You mean you didn't find out anything?" Doree demanded.

Spring's spirits dropped, and she slumped onto a kitchen chair. Their mother's life might depend on this information. "You mean we've hit a dead end already?"

"In a way, yes. In a way, no." Hannah slid another two sheets into the oven and set the timer. "This would be so much easier if we didn't have to keep it from Mother."

"Don't be irritating." Using red rope licorice and Red Hots, Doree began carefully crafting a face on her gingerbread boy.

Spring's worry had turned to dread. She had to know the truth. She made herself pick up a cookie to frost. "Just tell us."

Hannah sighed. "A few days after we'd settled in here, one night late, I went into Dad's office and opened the file that holds all the family records."

"Yes," Doree prompted, and bit off the head of the first gingerbread boy she'd decorated.

Hannah frowned at her. "But after I found the birth certificate, Dad walked in!"

"Oh, no." Spring put down the cookie she was frosting.

"What did you tell him?" Doree demanded.

"The truth, of course. He caught me red-handed."

"What did he say?" Spring asked. All the sweetness in the air was beginning to cloy in her throat.

"After I told him I was looking for Mom's natural parents and why," Hannah went on, "he explained why the natural parents' names weren't on the birth certificate. Then he said he did have some information that our grandmother gave him on her deathbed about Mother's birth."

"He did!" This surprised Spring. She popped up again, unable to sit still.

"So what was the information?" Doree insisted.

"He said that he couldn't violate Mother's wishes—"

"Oh." Doree groaned.

Hannah continued. "Unless he prayed about it and felt that it was right to go against Mother's—"

The outside door opened, letting in a rush of cold air.

Spring, pacing the floor, spun around. "Father!"

"I thought so." Her father took off his gloves and unwound his navy-blue scarf. "It smells delicious in here."

Going against Mother and Father wasn't something Spring had decided to do lightly. And now, with her father's unexpected return, she felt as though she'd been found with her hand in the cookie jar. "What did you think, Father?"

"I thought you three would be talking about your mother, so I came back—"

"Where'd you leave Mom?" Doree asked.

Father, the local pastor, sat down at the table with them. "I asked her to type something for me at the church office. I have to go back in a few minutes, then we'll head to Portage for her blood checkup." He picked up an unfrosted cookie and took a bite.

"Dad, have you changed your mind?" Hannah set down the dough she'd been flouring to roll out.

Dad nodded, then finished swallowing his first bit of gingerbread. He reached for Spring's hand and drew her to the chair beside him.

"Don't keep us guessing! What do you know, Dad?" Doree persisted.

"First, dear Doree, I want you to know I've decided to tell you all the information I have." He waited till all eyes had turned to him. "Your grandmother Gloria, who adopted your mother, wanted me to have the information about Ethel's birth mother because she said Ethel someday might want or need to know about her birth.''

Hannah nodded while Doree bit her lower lip.

Spring's anxiety surged inside her. Mother's leukemia was in remission now, but would it last? If it hadn't been for this disease, they wouldn't have to delve into the past. They wouldn't need to find possible bone marrow donors for her.

Father went on. ''Your grandmother told me two facts about your mother's birth. She told me that her natural mother died from complications of the birth and that her name was Connie Wilson.''

Shock zinged through Spring. ''Connie Wilson?''

Everyone turned to look at her.

Father asked, ''Is that name familiar to you?''

With surprise shimmering through her, Spring sat up straighter. ''Yes, I know who Connie Wilson was.''

Chapter One

The semi-truck's air brakes screamed in protest, and the huge cab bounced as it slowed to miss Great-Aunt Geneva's 1985 gold-toned Cadillac. Spring's heart stopped, then surged into an inner cacophony.

Without turning a hair, Aunt Geneva completed her illegal left turn across two lanes of bumper-to-bumper traffic.

"All these tourists! The northern 'sunbirds' have arrived for the winter." Aunt Geneva shook her tinted blond-over-gray head. Wearing a purple linen suit with her customary double shoulder pads, Aunty sat at the wheel like the captain of a cabin cruiser. "The traffic around here gets worse and worse all the time. And half of them never learned how to drive in the first place."

Spring's heart still thumped sickeningly. *Dear Lord, get us to the country club alive. I should have insisted on driving.* Out her window, the turquoise-blue waters of the Gulf of Mexico beckoned Spring in vain. The soft, warm breeze flowed in through the car window and over her face. As she kept an eye on the six lanes of traffic on Highway 19, she ran her fingers through her long hair, trying to keep the wind from tangling it.

"I'm just so thrilled that you've come to visit!" Aunt Geneva repeated for the umpteenth time, taking her eyes off the road to smile at Spring.

"You're making me feel guilty," Spring murmured nervously, eyeing the intimidating cement truck traveling beside her. "I come every year."

"But only for a week in February! This year I have you for three whole months in Gulfview! It will be just like having you at the university again." Aunty sounded her horn, swerved into the left lane, then cut in front of a bus.

Desperately holding onto her composure, Spring nodded. "I'm looking forward to it, too." She swallowed to moisten her dry mouth. "January, February and March in Milwaukee can sometimes be so…grim."

"I know, my dear, I spent many dreary years there."

"But Milwaukee's a fun town, and I'm near my parents—" Spring squeaked, "Red light!"

Aunty obligingly squealed to a halt.

Flying forward against her seat belt, then back against the seat, Spring hoped she hadn't suffered whiplash.

"Well, you were with them for Christmas. I loved

the pictures you brought of Ethel's new house. At last, she has the house she's always deserved.''

Spring wondered had she applied enough deodorant this morning? The warmth of the day and her aunt's fearless driving style was putting hers to the test!

''Now, don't get me wrong. Your father is a wonderful man, but Ethel hasn't always had everything just as I would have wanted it for her. The clergy don't bring in the bucks.''

''At least, none they can spend in this world,'' Spring pointed out gently. Why hadn't she offered to drive? How could she have forgotten her aunt's kamikaze driving style?

''Exactly so.'' Aunt Geneva nodded. ''But she does have you three girls, and you mean the world to her.''

Thinking of her sisters made Spring recall her mother and the leukemia. Spring's worry swelled within her. Would she and her sisters really be able to discover their mother's biological parents?

Even before her father had mentioned Connie Wilson during her Christmas at her parents' home, Spring had planned to spend time in Florida with Great-Aunt Geneva. Spring had taken a leave of absence from the Milwaukee Botanical Gardens to come to Florida for a few months to help Aunt Geneva, now in her late eighties, make the move to a retirement home.

The name, Connie Wilson, had rung a bell in Spring's mind—a moment during a visit to Aunt Geneva years ago. Had her memory been correct? Would Aunt Geneva have more clues for them?

"Penny for your thoughts, dear."

Spring couldn't bring herself to ask this most pressing question so early in the trip. Getting information about Connie Wilson might take some finesse. Something from the past warned Spring that this was true.

Piloting her massive sedan around a broad corner to a quieter local street, Aunt Geneva left the crush of traffic behind. Before Florida had boomed in the late eighties, her aunt's adventurous driving style hadn't been so dangerous. But now…

Breathing a sigh of relief, Spring recognized Bougainvillea Avenue, which would take them to her aunt's longtime country club. "Is the retirement home near Golden Sands?"

"No, no, dear, I have a little surprise for you. We have to stop for a brief meeting here first. Then we'll go on to tour the retirement home. Though, since you've come, I already feel twenty years younger."

Spring didn't return a comment on this "little surprise" of her aunt's. She was different from her sisters. Doree would have made some outrageous quip. And before Hannah had ever left the house, she would have asked for an itemized itinerary, but Spring just relaxed against the velour seat. Aunt Geneva always had a plan and she always got her way! Why fight it?

Aunty's car surged up the long drive to the venerable country club past bountiful azalea bushes, decorated with blossoms in every shade of pink imaginable, lining the way. Seagulls squawked overhead and the scent of the salty Gulf of Mexico spiced the air. Spring closed her eyes, savoring the moment. *Thank you, Lord, for bringing us safely here.*

The car jerked to a halt. A uniformed valet stepped out from under the canopied entrance. "*Señora* Dorfman, good afternoon. A lovely day."

The young Hispanic man, no doubt a college student still on break from school, helped her aunt out of the deep cushiony seat, then drove the car away to park it in the covered lot.

Aunty marched away with military straightness and purpose. Aunty had served in the WACs, the Women's Army Corps, in the Second World War and her gait still showed this.

Spring hurried to keep up with her, as they entered the low, rambling club. Only one-story high, painted white with graceful verandas on all sides, Golden Sands had been established before 1940 and still retained its southern charm. Palm trees and red hibiscus basked in the sun. Florida "tacky" had never been permitted within its gates.

Spring wondered what the surprise was and what meeting they would be attending. Aunty had served on every committee here at one time or another. But safely out of the car now and walking into the familiar building lulled Spring into a lush, dreamlike contentment. Two of Aunty's many friends waved to them from a round table on the veranda. Aunty steered Spring to meet them.

"We thought we'd meet out here, dahlings," Eleanor in her floral-print rayon dress said, smiling.

Though Eleanor had lived in Florida for more than thirty years, she still retained a touch of a New York accent.

"Yes, we're so happy the weather decided to behave for your visit, hon." Verna Rae, born and raised in Tampa, had a soft southern burr to her voice.

"You look lovely in that shade of pink, Spring. Like a princess." Eleanor squeezed Spring's hand in greeting.

"You're prettier than ever, but we've got to help you get your tan started, honey. You're so pale." Looking over her half-glasses for reading, a gold chain dangling over both ears, Verna Rae examined Spring from head to toe.

After greeting both the ladies with affectionate kisses, Spring sat down with her back to the club, so she could view the vast green golf course beyond the veranda. "You ladies know I've always been pale."

"When we were girls, we would have killed for such creamy skin like yours, dahling." Eleanor nodded. "But after the war, everybody started wanting a tan. Now they say skin cancer. Always wear sunblock, and they talk numbers. My granddaughter won't let her little one out without number thirty. That's what she tells me the doctor told her. Do you wear number thirty, too?"

Spring smiled. "Yes, otherwise I burn."

"Well, maybe you ought to lower that number and get a little color, honey. I've had a tan for forty years and no skin cancer. I like a healthy glow on a young girl like you." Against the white cotton duck of her slacks and short-sleeved top, Verna Rae's skin resembled tanned leather.

Spring would have died before commenting on this, so she just smiled. "I'm sure I'll pick up some color while I'm here. That Florida sun won't let me get away untouched." *I'll get my usual million tiny golden freckles!* "Are we all here, then?"

"We have one more member coming—" Eleanor said.

"Yes, we thought we'd like the man's point of view." Verna Rae gave a decisive nod of her head.

A man's point of view? "On what?" Spring asked.

"On the April Garden Show, of course. Didn't I tell you?" Aunty looked honestly surprised.

But her cat in the cream expression was reflected in the other two ladies' faces. Spring didn't like the sound of this. Was this the surprise, then, having her at the garden show meeting? Or was the other shoe about to drop?

"Do you still have one each year?" She didn't want to organize a garden show! That's what she did all the time at the Milwaukee Botanical Gardens— plan different types of shows, exhibits, always new ideas to draw in people and contributions to the gardens. *I'm on vacation!* She felt like fleeing to the nearest exit.

"Oh!" Aunty exclaimed, looking over Spring's head. "Here's our last member. Good morning, Dr. Da Palma."

"Good morning to you, Mrs. Dorfman," a voice, deep and rich, replied.

Spring instantly recognized that once-familiar voice and froze where she sat. *It can't be.*

A tanned hand pulled out the chair beside her and a long, lean man in a light tan suit sat down.

The hair on the back of her neck prickled. Slowly she lifted her eyes to his face.

It was him. Even though she hadn't seen him for years, she'd recognize Marco Da Palma's classically handsome face anywhere. Why are you here, Marco? Their eyes met and shock after shock lapped through her.

"Why…" He stared at her. "Spring Kirkland?"

Nodding like a puppet, she held out her nerveless hand. "Marco, how…how good to see you."

Aunty beamed at them. "I thought you two had attended university together."

"Yes, I had the pleasure of taking a few undergraduate classes with your niece, Mrs. Dorfman." Marco smiled.

In Marco's presence, Aunty, Eleanor and Verna Rae perked up visibly, while Spring willed herself to remain and look calm. Did her panic show on her face? Meeting him again like this!

"Are you down for your yearly visit?" Marco asked.

Spring gave a little start. How did Marco know she visited Aunt Geneva every February? She hadn't seen him since graduation. "No…this year I'm here for a longer visit." Stilling her inner tremors she drew herself up straighter. "My aunt wants my help to move into a retirement home."

"A retirement home?" Marco studied Aunt Geneva for a moment. "You hadn't mentioned that to me during your recent checkup."

Check-up? Spring tried to make sense of this remark.

Aunty fiddled with the many lavish rings on her fingers. "I thought it might be advisable to look into the possibility...at my age, you know."

Verna Rae and Eleanor both looked away, suddenly vitally interested in a group of retired men at the golf course tee nearest them.

Spring tried to guess what was going on among the three older ladies, but Marco's presence was playing havoc with her mind.

Marco said, "Don't forget to come in for your blood-pressure check, Mrs. Dorfman."

Spring frowned. "I didn't know you were my aunt's physician, Marco."

"I am." He nodded his head at each of the three older ladies around the table. "I took over most of Dr. Johnson's practice when he retired two years ago."

"And we're so happy you did," Eleanor crooned. "It's such a nice thing. To go to someone who we saw grow up right before our eyes. I'd hate to have to tell a stranger all about my ailments."

"That's right, hon," Verna Rae agreed. "Marco has been part of this club since he was a groundskeeper's assistant in the summers. What were you when you started? Fourteen?"

Marco nodded.

Spring thought it was a stiff nod. Now that Marco was a doctor, did he prefer not to remember the years he spent working at Golden Sands? He'd always struck her as a proud man. She hoped the ladies hadn't pierced him with their well-intentioned words. Evidently, as a successful Golden Sands scholarship student, he'd been offered a membership after graduation.

She took a deep breath, pushing away all the memories that seeing Marco had evoked. "Perhaps we should get the meeting started? I'm sure Marco is a busy man."

"Well, so was Jack and you know what happened to him?" Eleanor said in a teasing tone.

"Jack?" Spring couldn't think what the lady was alluding to.

"The Jack who did all work and no play." Eleanor waggled a finger at them. "A very dull boy was Jack."

The meeting went downhill from there—in Spring's opinion. The day of the garden show had been set for the second Saturday in April. The three ladies brought out the notes kept by last year's committee.

Beside her, Marco appeared interested—but was it pretense? She felt for him. She didn't doubt for a moment that he'd been "guilted" into coming. Marco had been one of the many students who'd benefited from Golden Sands scholarships and employment. He was the kind of man to repay debts, even if they included garden club meetings.

She'd frozen into a polite pose and couldn't even make small talk. The points of the discussion slipped past her. All she was aware of was the clean line of Marco's profile and the citrus fragrance of his after-shave.

"Spring, dahling," Eleanor prompted. "Aren't you feeling well? You haven't said two words."

Her already warm face blazed. "I'm sorry. I don't seem able to concentrate. Maybe it's the change from winter to summer. I just can't get my thoughts to-gether."

Eleanor gave her a knowing wink.

"I think we've done enough today," Verna Rae said smoothly, folding up the file from last year's event. "We'll meet again next week. Same time. Same place."

"I'll try to attend," Marco said as he rose. "But I think I will be on call for the hospital that day. If an emergency comes up..." He shrugged, then turned to go.

"Why don't you walk me and my niece to the door?" Aunt Geneva stood up.

Spring cringed at this ploy. *I can get there by my-self!* But she couldn't demur. It would be too impo-lite.

"My pleasure." Marco helped Spring out of her chair. His hand brushed her bare arm, and she tingled with the contact.

"We are going to drop by that retirement home on Azalea Drive." Aunty marched toward the entrance, with Marco and Spring on her right.

"I've heard good things about that retirement home." Marco glanced at Spring.

Marco's nearness tightening her throat, Spring concentrated on putting one foot in front of the other.

"Yes, yes. It's supposed to be lovely." Aunt Geneva lifted her chin.

At the entrance, Marco waited with them for the valet to bring out the car. When it arrived, Spring tried to get a turn at the wheel herself. Her aunt insisted she knew the way to the retirement home and ended up behind the wheel again. He held back a smile, knowing full well why Spring wanted to drive. Mrs. Dorfman's Wild West driving was notorious around the club. Spring must have nerves of steel.

Spring Kirkland. More lovely than ever. He began to think over the possibilities. Maybe she would be of some help.

Chapter Two

"Now this is one of our deluxe suites." The tall elegant man with silver at his temples smiled as he ushered Aunty and Spring through the door.

Spring hung back and let her aunt take the lead. The sitting room stretched in front of them, done in shades of ivory and sea-foam green with touches of polished brass. A sliding glass door at one end overlooked a garden where seniors sat chatting and some playing cards around shaded tables.

Spring turned her gaze back to her aunt. Her nerves still quivered from seeing Marco again.

"Ah," Aunty murmured as she scanned the room.

"Of course, you can redecorate to your own taste. This is the only one I have to show you now. We keep pretty full."

Spring frowned. Why had her aunt and friends decided to drag Marco into garden show meetings, of

all things? Had they been matchmaking or just trying
to liven up the meetings?

Aunty nodded to the man, then walked through another door into the bedroom with its adjoining bath.

A dreadful thought occurred to Spring. Could
Marco possibly have thought *she'd* asked for him to
be included on the committee for her sake? She
cringed inside.

The gentleman followed Aunt Geneva, pointing out
the bed that adjusted like a hospital bed for comfort,
then pointed to grip bars added for safety in the bath.

Spring brushed aside her preoccupation with Marco
and what he thought of the meeting, or of seeing her
again. What could she do about it now? She'd just
have to make certain she remained outwardly com-
posed. Marco had shown nothing but politeness at
seeing her again. She would follow his lead, no matter
how his presence affected her.

The gentleman trailed Aunty back out into the sitting room again. "Do you have any more questions?"

"No, I went over your literature before, at home."

Forcing her mind back to the present, Spring tried
to gauge her aunt's reaction to the retirement suite,
but Aunty was giving no clear indication of what she
was thinking. Aunty said the right things and looked
like a prospective tenant, but…

The gentleman cleared his throat. "I don't want to
seem forward, but we don't have vacancies very often. If you're interested, let us know as soon as you
make a decision. I have two more couples looking at
this suite today."

Aunty nodded. "I will. Thank you for your time." The tour came to its natural end, and Spring walked beside Aunt Geneva to the front, where Aunty had parked her car in the shade of a live oak.

Wondering why the tour had struck her as not quite right, Spring asked again to take the driver's seat.

"You still don't like my driving, do you," Aunty replied with a wry smile.

"Let's say, I'm not quite as adventurous at the wheel as you are. Besides, I enjoy driving a cabin cruiser through town."

Chuckling at this familiar answer, Aunt Geneva sighed as she eased into the passenger seat. She handed over the key. "You're a good girl, Spring."

"You're a good aunt." Spring looked over and glimpsed a strange expression on her aunt's face. "Are you feeling all right?"

"Of course, I am. That doesn't mean I don't have aches and pains. You can't live to almost ninety without those. More's the pity."

Spring felt guilty. She'd been so busy thinking about Mother and about Marco that she'd been ignoring her great-aunt's dilemma. The prospect of leaving her home of more than thirty years must be painful. "Why are you thinking of moving into a retirement community or residence? Do you feel the house is too much for you to handle now?"

Aunty avoided her gaze. "I don't know. I just thought I should look around and see what is available. You're the closest thing I have to a daughter. I don't have any family here in Florida and I've seen other retirees wait too long to make a graceful move to a retirement community. I'm trying to decide if now is the right time for me to move or should I wait.''

"I see.'' Spring had disappointed her aunt by not settling in the Sunshine State after college. It had been a difficult decision to make, since Aunt Geneva had paid for Spring's childhood operations to correct a clubfoot, then later for college—even the money to pledge a sorority.

But at graduation, she'd gotten an offer from the prestigious Milwaukee Botanical Gardens while her sister, Doree, had still been a school girl at home in Milwaukee. After being away for four years, Spring had wanted to spend time with Doree before she left their parents' nest.

"Why don't we stop at Joan's and see if she has anything that will catch your eye?'' Aunty suggested.

Spring wanted to decline. She had more than enough clothing in her closet at home, but Aunty loved to take her shopping. Buying beautiful outfits for Spring had constituted one of Aunt Geneva's greatest pleasures since Spring was six.

Her asthma had been bad that winter, and her parents had sent her to Aunt Geneva's house for a winter of sun and convalescence. Having no children of her own to spoil, Aunt Geneva had showered Spring with gifts and was still delighted to do so.

Spring grinned. "Sounds like fun to me.''

Aunty's face broke into a broad smile. "Wonderful!''

Soon Spring parked in front of a trendy strip mall in an exclusive section of town. As they strolled into the boutique, Joan, the owner, greeted them. "My two favorite customers! You're here for a long visit, Spring?"

Shopping with Aunty always summoned up childhood memories of the lovely clothes Aunty had sent to Spring so generously. In turn, Hannah had accepted the hand-me-downs without complaint. But of course Doree had flatly refused to touch them! If Doree were here now, she'd certainly be angry that Spring hadn't immediately broached the subject of their mother's biological family. But the right time just hadn't presented itself.

Before long, Spring walked out of the dressing room in a rose silk sheath. Aunty sat in a split-bamboo chair near the three-way mirror. With her back to it, Spring posed gracefully. "What do you think, Aunty?"

Aunt Geneva studied her. "Turn."

Spring obeyed in a practiced motion.

"What do you think?" Aunty asked her.

I wish I didn't have a mission to carry out. I wish I could just relax and enjoy myself. But Spring, centered in front of the mirror, examined herself critically from all angles. "It fits well."

"Do you like it?" Aunty asked.

"Not enough to buy it." Spring had been so certain that she'd heard the name Connie Wilson from her aunt's lips. But maybe she was wrong. She'd only been about twelve when she'd come upon that pho-

tograph of Aunt Geneva, her only sister, Gloria, and
their childhood friend. Had the friend's name really
been Connie Wilson?

The process continued. Spring finally tried on a
three-piece peach linen ensemble. In front of the mirror, she announced, "I can't resist."

"Your gold herringbone chains and bracelet would
be just the thing for it," Aunty agreed with a dazzling
smile.

Spring nodded and Joan beamed in satisfaction.
Spring walked out with the outfit carefully folded in
gold tissue paper and tucked into a long gold-and-
white box, tied with gold curling ribbon.

"That's just the kind of outfit you need for that
University of Florida alumni cruise." Without argument this time, Aunty eased herself into the passenger
seat.

Spring wondered if the morning had tired Aunty.
"I had that in mind when I selected it. It's going to
be fun, seeing all my college friends again." Would
Marco be going, too? *Where had that thought come
from?*

"I wonder if Dr. Da Palma will be going on the
cruise, too."

"I don't know." Having Aunty put her thoughts
into words shook Spring. She was going to have to
be very careful around Aunty and her friends. Why
did older women take it as their duty to try to match
everyone into pairs?

"You'll have to ask him at the next meeting. A
cruise is just what he needs. He's an excellent doctor,

but he doesn't seem to have any life apart from his practice. He should be looking for a wife."

Spring acted as though this didn't matter to her at all. "That's just like him. I mean, that was how he was in college." And she'd had to accept it then.

Evidently he hadn't changed.

"Marco, you're not paying attention." His petite mother nudged him. "Are you done eating?"

From his seat at the round table in the dinette just off the kitchen, he glanced up. "Sorry, Mama. Just a long day." He could hardly admit to himself that he'd been remembering how elegant Spring Kirkland had looked at the garden show meeting.

"Well, I'm glad you stopped here for dinner or you'd probably have skipped another meal."

"Believe me, when I get hungry, I eat." Marco finished the last bit of the spicy casserole. He wiped his mouth with his paper napkin and pushed his plate and silverware aside. "Okay, Paloma, get out that calculus and we'll get it done."

"Don't call me that name!" His teenage half-sister twisted her face in a heartfelt grimace.

"It's your name, *little dove*." Marco teased her with the translation of her Spanish name, one that had been in her father's family for generations.

"I'm just Maria, okay?" She ducked around the corner, then returned with her book and notebook. His sister had taken a recent dislike to the family name her father had insisted she have, and she'd announced she would be called by her middle name, Maria.

"Why don't you want to be distinctive? There are millions of Maria's, but very few Paloma's." Two weeks ago, Paloma had decided to change her name. So far she'd had very little luck in changing her family's mind. Had someone at school teased her about her name? If she kept this up, he'd have to delve deeper and see what was bothering her.

Their mother shook her head at them and left with Marco's dishes in her hands. Paloma wiped the table with a napkin, then spread her textbook and notebook in front of her brother. "I'm having trouble with these four problems."

For the next twenty minutes, Marco and his sister went over her assignment. Then the back door opened and shut. "I'm home!" The cheerful voice of his stepfather, Santos, boomed in the kitchen. His mother's laughter greeted her husband.

Marco and Paloma looked up, as Santos walked into the dinette. "Marco, *hola,* did you have a good day?"

Marco nodded, glancing at the barrel-chested man who had married his mother when Marco was fourteen.

"I see our girl needs more help with her math." Santos, a plumber, rolled up the sleeves of his khaki work shirt to wash for his late supper.

"We're just finishing up." Marco looked at his sister. "You've got that now?"

"Sure. At least, for today. I just hope it sticks for the test." Paloma made a face.

"Your brother has set you a good example. No

going out with friends this weekend if that test score isn't good.'' Santos shook his finger at her.

Paloma frowned. ''I know.''

Wishing Santos wouldn't always wave Marco's success in his little sister's face, Marco rose and lifted his sports jacket from the back of his chair. ''I think it's time I went home.''

''You don't have to run off like that,'' Santos objected.

''I've got some patient notes to look over and early rounds at the hospital.''

''You need to learn to relax a little now, son. You have earned the right to enjoy yourself.''

''Medicine is a twenty-four hours a day, seven days a week kind of job.''

''Then, you doctors need a better union,'' Santos joked.

Marco nodded politely to his stepfather and walked out to his car. As he drove away, his mother stood at the kitchen window, waving goodbye.

Loneliness snaked through him. Santos was a good man. His mother was happy, and Paloma was a treasure. But he'd never felt at home in that house. His family really had ended with his father's death, and nothing could change that. Or, at least, nothing ever had.

Then Spring Kirkland's lovely face flickered in his memory, as it often had in the days since he'd seen her again—after all the years apart. He'd meant to call her to ask for her help, but every time he stood with the receiver in his hand, he ended up putting it down without calling. What would he say?

"Spring?" Hannah's voice came over the phone line.

Trying to suppress her nervousness, Spring settled back in the chair beside her bed, but she couldn't stop herself from accusing. "Hi, you didn't call me when you said you would."

"I'm sorry. I've been really busy. Deadline frenzy with my new cookbook." Hannah sounded stressed.

"Did you find out about Mother's latest blood work?" Spring asked.

"I was going to call you last night, but I forgot you're an hour earlier than we are—"

"What did the test reveal?" Spring interrupted.

"It wasn't as good as the doctor had hoped, but he said not to worry."

Easy for him to say. Hannah's worried. I'm worried. "Is Father upset?"

"He says he'll just continue to pray."

Of course, prayer is what we all are doing, but why don't I feel comforted? Spring tried to think what to say. "How's Guthrie?"

"Wonderful."

Spring couldn't think of anything more to say and guessed that her sister felt the same. The dread over their mother's health had silenced their usual chatter.

Spring started, "I'll call soon—"

"Have you asked Aunt—"

"I will."

"All right. Good night."

"Good night." Spring put down the receiver. *No more waiting for the right time. Tomorrow I ask Aunt Geneva about Connie Wilson.*

Suppressing a yawn from lack of sleep, Spring stood on the patio outside her aunt's sweeping Florida room, the all-season porch that spanned the rear of the house. Beyond the patio, palm trees stood like sentinels above her aunt's lush garden, and beyond the fence, the azure Gulf. Spring took up her box of well-used pastels and contemplated the blank paper on her easel. She hadn't had time to draw for nearly six months. She didn't really feel like it now, but she'd decided this would take them out of the house, away from her aunt's housekeeper, Matilde. Whatever was said, she wanted to keep the secrets surrounding her mother's birth private.

"You make such a picture standing there." Aunt Geneva sat in the shade of the roof with her knitting in her lap.

Spring glanced down at her white shorts and pale yellow shirt—nothing special. Once again, she tried to come up with a way of introducing the subject of her mother's natural parents. Her mind was a blank.

"What should I sketch today? Something I can see or something inside my mind?"

"Suit yourself, dear." Her aunt's needles clicked, weaving pale pink baby yarn together into a knit cap for a newborn at the nearby hospital.

Spring stood there, wondering which to do. Worry

over her mother's illness and her own timidity about asking Aunty "the question" capped any creative energy she possessed. In default mode, she selected blue and began to stroke a fine layer of blue chalk over the top half of the paper on the easel. *Just say it!* "Aunty, you know about Mother's illness...."

"Yes, dear, I've been so thankful for her remission. What would your father do without her? Ethel has always been the practical one. I wonder if your father has ever realized how lucky he's been in having a wife like Ethel."

"I'm sure he has—"

"Well, he better, that's all I can say."

Spring glanced over her shoulder at Aunty. How could she just ask—out of the blue like this? Taking a deep breath, she began the foundation for the big question. "You know, before she went into remission, the doctor said that she might need a bone marrow donor. All three of us girls were tested, but none of us was a match."

"Uh-huh." Aunty appeared to be counting stitches.

Spring gazed skyward, gathering momentum. "That was a great worry to us. I mean, what if Mother had reached the point where she needed a donor and none of us could help her?"

"I see." The needles started clicking again. "But that didn't happen."

"But it might have. It might happen in the future."

"But Ethel is in remission!"

The moment had come. No more beating around the bush. "Aunty, my sisters and I want, need—"

"*Señora* Dorfman, Paloma has come." Plump Matilde, with her salt-and-pepper gray hair in a bun, ambled out through the Florida room to the patio, her arthritis slowing her. A pretty girl who had long black hair and wore blue jeans and a red T-shirt trailed behind her.

Spring paused and turned. Matilde had been her aunt's housekeeper for the past thirty years. She'd spoiled Spring right along with her aunt. But right now, when she'd just worked up the courage to ask her aunt THE question—she wished Matilde anywhere pleasant but here.

"Excellent." Aunt Geneva smiled. "Hello, Paloma. So you're going to start helping Matilde out on the weekends?"

"Yes, ma'am." The young girl looked up shyly.

Aunt Geneva motioned toward Spring. "This is my niece, Spring."

"What a pretty name." The girl glanced at Spring, then seemed to freeze, gazing at her.

Spring hated it when people stared, but she merely returned the girl's regard. The Hispanic girl's face was lovely, fresh, her expression so winsome. "I'd love to paint you." The words popped out of Spring's mouth.

"Oh! I..." The girl blushed.

I've embarrassed her. Spring had forgotten how sensitive teenage girls could be.

"Oh, that would be wonderful." Matilde clapped her hands. "Her *quinceañería* is in just a few months, the end of April. It would be a wonderful gift for her parents!''

''What's a quinceañería?'' Spring asked.

''It's her fifteenth birthday, a special occasion in a girl's life. The custom comes from Mexico, where her father was born. I went to school with her father, Santos.''

''But I'm here to work,'' Paloma said quietly, looking from one to the other of the three ladies.

''Well, you can sit for me briefly in between your chores,'' Spring suggested.

''Excellent!'' Aunt Geneva beamed.

''*Bueno,*'' Matilde agreed.

''Come sit here in this chair,'' Spring instructed as she pulled a wicker chair into place. The sun would come over the girl's shoulder and cast interesting shadows over her face.

The front door chimes rang out. ''I'll go get that.'' Matilde hurried away, favoring her bad knee.

Spring arranged the ill-at-ease girl in the wicker chair. ''With the garden behind you, this is going to be lovely.''

''But I'm in work clothes. I—''

''Today I'll just begin. I just need to look at you and study your face and form. When we get to the clothing, you can bring something else to pose in.'' Spring lifted the girl's chin to the right and left, trying to decide which was her best side.

''*Señora,* it's the doctor.'' Matilde stood aside at the doorway.

At these mundane words, Spring spun around. *Marco! Here?*

Marco walked in, carrying a small black bag.

The sight of him in a crisp dark suit sent a sharp zigzag of excitement through Spring. All the years away from him melted away.

Marco began in an all-business tone—unaware of Spring and oblivious of her marked reaction to him. "Mrs. Dorfman, you didn't come for your blood-pressure check—" He broke off, staring at his sister. "Paloma, what are you doing here?"

Aunty and Matilde turned to look at him.

Matilde recovered first. "Marco, your sister is going to start helping me on the weekends. I need another pair of hands on Saturday. And now Spring wants to draw her portrait for her *quinceañería*. A present to thank your parents!"

"Paloma, when did your father decide you needed to start working?" Marco demanded, glaring at her.

Marco's tone bothered Spring. He was overreacting. *What's going on?*

Paloma rose hesitantly. "I...I want to start saving for college. Matilde had mentioned that she'd be needing help...I..." The girl's voice died away.

Marco scowled.

Knowing Marco from years ago, Spring realized he was humiliated to have his sister working as domestic help. Marco's overly sensitive pride had been all too evident years ago and that had not changed.

"So, Doctor, you've chased me down," Aunty rallied. "I was planning on coming over early next week. Anyone would think I was at death's door—"

"I'm your doctor and I told you I wanted to monitor your blood pressure closely through this month. Now please take off your jacket and I'll get this done. I'm on my way to the hospital to check on some patients."

His sharp tone surprised Spring. *Please, Marco, don't be so upset.* Then an unwelcome thought intruded. What was so wrong with Aunty's blood pressure that Marco would come to the house?

Aunt Geneva followed his instructions, and he put the black cuff on her arm. Though unsettled by this development, Spring tried to act naturally. She motioned to Paloma to sit back down, then contemplated which color to use next.

The young girl looked uncomfortable and kept glancing at her brother. Spring smiled at her, trying to put her at her ease while she strove to ignore her own keen awareness of Marco.

"Well, how did I do?" Aunty asked tartly, when Marco finished.

Spring was silently asking the same question.

"You're still higher than I want you to be. I don't want to increase your blood-pressure medicine until I'm forced to. Have you started exercising, as you promised me?"

Aunt Geneva sighed. "No, I've been so busy—"

"Make time." Marco packed up his blood-pressure kit. "I expect to see you walking regularly and losing a few pounds."

"Yes, Doctor." Aunty grimaced.

Spring frowned. Was this what had prompted her aunt to think about retirement homes? She had to find out if her aunt's health really was declining, even if it meant putting herself in the path of Marco's unconscious yet risky charm.

"I'll be going now." Marco glanced at Spring.

She tried to read his expression but couldn't. "I'll walk you to your car. Paloma, why don't you go ahead and help Matilde, and when you're done come back to me."

Spring didn't give anyone a chance to object. She walked swiftly toward the house with Marco in her wake.

Outside, in front of her aunt's sprawling ranch, walking toward Marco's car, she asked, "Is my aunt's health something I should be concerned about?" She lowered her gaze to limit Marco's effect on her.

"I can't be specific, but let me tell you that I'm glad you're here. She needs someone who can get her to take better care of herself."

Spring worried her lower lip. "Is it her age?"

"Age is a factor, yes."

"She's always been so healthy, I think it's difficult for her—" *and for me* "—to accept the fact that she is finally feeling the effects of being nearly ninety."

"No doubt, that's correct. Now, make sure she comes to me twice next week."

"To save us a trip, could you check her blood pressure after the next garden show meeting?" Spring chanced a glance at him—suddenly glad that he was her aunt's doctor.

Marco pursed his lips. "I'm glad you brought that up. I need your help."

Spring lifted one eyebrow. "With what?"

Chapter Three

With Spring's lovely blue eyes gazing up at him so seriously, Marco felt as tongue-tied as a young boy. Why hadn't the years toughened him so that this beautiful, unattainable woman would no longer have the power to make him want to pull her close for a stolen kiss?

Spring Kirkland, I thought I'd completely forgotten you.

But his heart had played him for a fool again. He still wanted her. He still couldn't have her.

She touched his arm. Even through the double layer of fabric, shirt and jacket, her touch shocked him. He swallowed to moisten his dry mouth so he could answer her.

"What is it, Marco? You look so worried."

Get a grip, man. "I'm just…busy. When Dr. Johnson sold me his practice so reasonably, it was a great stroke of luck—"

"Don't you mean a blessing?" She let her hand drop to her side as she leaned gracefully against the car. Her long, slender legs stretched out in front of him.

He couldn't take his eyes off her. Didn't she realize what an enticing picture she made? Why hadn't some successful Anglo man married her by now? He hung onto the thread of their conversation. "A blessing, yes. But taking on a full practice right away brought huge responsibilities with it."

She folded her slim arms in front of her. The sunlight glinted off the diamond tennis bracelet she wore.

He steeled himself against her allure. "I joined Golden Sands so I could contribute to the club's scholarship program, which had been a godsend to me. But I've never really used the membership. I've been hoping you could help me."

She nodded, encouraging him.

"I'm not the country-club type and I don't have time to waste on garden show meetings. I've been wanting to ask you for days—can you think of a polite way of getting me out of them?"

"I see. You want me to help you resign from the committee?" She pursed her lips. "You're wasting your time?"

"It's not that I'm ungrateful for all that Golden Sands did for me. Without working there and without the club's generous scholarships, as a fatherless immigrant from the Dominican Republic, I wouldn't have been able to finish college without a crushing load of debt, but..." He pushed one hand through his hair, hating to voice so much of his history of need. "I just think my time would be better spent doing what my education prepared me to do—medicine."

Her long, golden hair flowing over her shoulders and veiling her face, she looked down at the asphalt drive. "You were upset to see your sister working with Matilde?"

The question, so off the subject, threw him. "What?"

"You don't want your sister to work for my aunt." She glanced up at him, her lovely face so intense.

He tried to read her expression but couldn't. How had she known how embarrassed he'd been? "I just don't think it's necessary for her to work right now." The words sounded stiff even to his own ears.

"I think you have some seriously wrong ideas about my family." She tossed her hair back from her face.

Her totally unexpected words, along with her undeniable attractiveness, left him in confusion. He clung to the topic at hand. "What has that got to do with what we're talking about?"

"A great deal." She pushed away from the car. "I'll let you get back to your *busy* practice."

Unable to stop himself, he turned as he watched her saunter away. He'd obviously had no effect on her! "Will you help me?"

"I'll consider what you've told me."

He couldn't make himself move until he'd followed her with his gaze all the way into the sprawling white house. When she shut the double doors behind her, her spell over him was finally broken, and he slid into his car and drove away.

Something had happened between him and Spring just now, but what? Why had she spoken of his sister? And what did she mean *he* had seriously wrong ideas?

"Aunty?" Spring tapped on her aunt's bedroom door that night.

"Come in, dear."

Spring stepped inside and closed the door behind her. Ever since Marco had visited early in the day, she had turned over and over in her mind what he'd said to her, along with what she still needed to ask her aunt—plus her own turbulent feelings about both. Right now, though, she'd decided to concentrate on the question she'd been sent by her sisters to ask. That was the most important.

Dressed for bed in a flowing lavender caftan, Aunt Geneva reclined on her chaise longue by the window, knitting another bootie. "What is it, dear? You look worried."

In her pale pink pajamas, Spring perched on the chair near her aunt. "There's something I need to ask you. You may not want to give me the information, but I hope—we all hope—you will."

Aunty's eyebrows rose above her reading glasses. "This sounds very serious."

"It is." Spring gripped the arms of her chair.

Aunty removed her glasses and set them, along with her knitting, on the small table beside her. "Does it have to do with Marco?"

"Marco?" The thought startled Spring. "This has nothing to do with Marco. Aunty, I—"

"Why aren't you married yet?"

Spring gawked at her aunt. "Marriage isn't the subject I wanted to talk to you about—"

"Well, this is the conversation I've intended to have with you for a long time now. You are always so distant and cool around men. You never flirt or use your beauty in any way I can detect. You just don't seem to know how to attract a man. Why not?" Her aunt stared at her.

Spring tried not to react to her aunt's bald words, but they echoed too closely the things her sisters had been telling her for years. That awful sinking feeling slid through her. No one understood the pressures she'd faced.

"Aunty—"

"You're beautiful!" Aunty flung her hands wide. "I should be fighting like a lioness to protect you. Men should be following you around like lovesick puppies—"

"Stop!" Spring pressed her hands to her warming face. Tears threatened to overflow. "I don't want men around me…acting like lovesick puppies or…vulgar idiots!" Unwelcome images and words from the past crowded Spring's mind, especially that night on campus that Marco had come to her rescue. She willed herself to block out the unpleasant sensations these memories carried with them. Goose bumps crawled up her arms.

"Dear, sweet child." Swinging her legs over the

side of her chaise longue, Aunty sat up and clasped her hands around Spring's small wrists. "Tell me what has upset you. Please."

Slowly Spring lowered her hands, but she averted her face.

Aunt Geneva let her own hands drop to her lap. "Tell me. Be honest."

Spring drew in a shuddering breath. "I don't like *that...kind* of attention from men." She shivered. "I don't like it when they get close to me and...say things to me when they don't think anyone else can hear."

"You mean...sexual comments?"

"Sometimes...vulgar insinuations." Spring's face blazed as she recalled some of these, still vivid in her memory. "They act like I'm not a real person...like I'm just a face, a body...."

"You poor dear." Aunty frowned. "Those kind of comments would wound someone like you, someone shy, especially someone raised like you were in a parsonage."

"What was wrong with the way I was raised? Mother and Father are wonderful parents!"

Aunty clenched her hands. "They are, but they never told you how beautiful you are or prepared you for the power beauty brings with it. They didn't warn you of the special demands of being so lovely—"

"You're not making any sense!" Spring hated this! She'd come in to ask about Connie Wilson, not to discuss her "beauty"!

"We should have had this conversation years ago!

I don't know why I didn't recognize this in you before. Now I can see how it all fits together.''

"What are you talking about?" *None of this fits together!*

Aunty leaned against the arm of her chaise. "You're kind of young to remember Marilyn Monroe, aren't you."

"You mean the movie star in the fifties?" Shaken, Spring couldn't understand where her aunt was heading with this.

"Yes, she was a beautiful young woman, but men never saw anything but her beautiful face and figure. She died young and all alone. A very sad story."

"What does that have to do with me?" Spring's temples started throbbing.

"Your parents being good Christians raised you to judge people not by their appearance, but by their value to God." Aunty gave her a knowing look.

"Of course, they did." *They taught me what was right.*

Aunty shook her head ruefully. "But most people judge by appearance only. Ethel and Garner should have taught you how to handle the extra attention you'd receive as a beauty, how to put men—rude men—in their place."

"You can learn that?" Spring stared at her aunt.

Aunty nodded. "If only I had realized, I could have helped you. Why didn't you say how much you were hurting?"

"I didn't think…I didn't know…"

"Sweetheart, we've got to do something about this.

I can't make you less sensitive, but I can help you come out of this shell you've built around yourself." Aunty took both Spring's hands in hers. "We can't let this spoil your life. You are the sweetest, kindest girl in the world, and we're going to get you over this, so you can find your one true love!"

My one true love. Longing swelled inside Spring. Her expression must have given her away.

"You are in love!"

"No, I—"

"Who is he?"

"Aunty—"

"Is it Marco?"

The rapid-fire questions overwhelmed Spring. Before she could stop herself, she nodded.

"Oh, but that's wonderful! Marco needs a woman like you in his life! He's just going to waste! You two would make a wonderful pair."

"Aunt Geneva, no!" Spring gasped, trying to rein in her aunt. "Marco isn't interested in me. He might be dating someone else—"

"No, I don't think he is, but we'll check with Matilde. How fortunate you two are both on the garden show committee."

"You didn't get him on the committee just because you knew I would be here—?"

"No." Aunt Geneva shrugged and made an apologetic moue. "We insisted he join us mainly because the man has no social life."

"Coming to garden show meetings would give him

a social life?'' The sweet foolishness of this plan released some of the tension Spring had been feeling.

''Of course not, but we decided it would get him
to the country club, and we would see what developed
from there.''

''Marco says he's too busy. He wants to get off—''

Aunt Geneva shook her head adamantly. ''Not a
chance. Marco has got to start having a life, not just
a career.''

Spring sighed. She felt beaten and shaken, as
though she had just run through a hailstorm. She still
hadn't posed the big question she'd come in to ask
Aunt Geneva. But she couldn't make herself bring up
another emotionally charged topic now. She rose and
kissed her aunt's soft cheek.

When she reached the door, her aunt's voice
stopped her. ''What did you come here to ask me?''

Spring shook her head, too weary now to take up
the task of asking her aunt about Connie Wilson.

''Now, don't you worry, dear. Tomorrow we'll begin bringing you out of your shell and into Marco's
much-too-serious life. Dr. Da Palma won't know what
hit him!''

Dazed, Spring walked out, feeling like a condemned woman. The possibilities for embarrassment
to both her and Marco loomed over her. Aunt Geneva
and friends were capable of anything! *Don't worry,
she says. Don't worry?*

The next morning, Spring and Aunty decided to
have their breakfast in the airy patio off the kitchen.

Warm sunshine, the rhythmic sound of the waves, and the call of gulls made an idyllic setting.

Still in her pink pajamas, Spring sighed, then rolled the tangy, fresh-squeezed ruby-red grapefruit juice over her tongue. "Thank you. I've dreamed about your breakfasts, Matilde."

"Matilde," Aunt Geneva in pink curlers and matching robe ordered, "sit down. We need to talk to you."

Spring prayed, *Please, Lord, don't let her—*

"My niece is interested in Marco."

Plump Matilde sat down, then bounced in her chair. "*Bueno, bueno.* Marco's mother will be thrilled—"

"Don't!" Spring held up her hand the way a crossing guard would. This was exactly what she'd dreaded! "Don't tell *anyone*, especially Marco's mother! Please!"

"Oh, *querida,* don't worry." Matilde patted her arm. "I meant only that his mother will be thrilled when you and Marco are engaged—"

"He isn't even interested in me!" Spring exclaimed.

"*Yet,*" Aunt Geneva pronounced. "Now, Matilde, I wanted to speak with you to make certain Marco has no romantic interest in anyone else."

"No, no, he's always working. Before he was always studying. His mother invites pretty girls to the house. She hints. But he's always too busy. She wants grandchildren—"

Spring bent and rested her forehead in her hand. "You're getting carried away." These women were transforming her college crush on Marco into future grandchildren!

One on each side of Spring, Aunt Geneva and Matilde patted her shoulders.

"Don't worry, Spring," Aunty replied. "You just need a little coaching."

Spring cringed. She'd have to think of something to keep this from spoiling her friendship with Marco and making fools of both of them.

Aunty again turned to her smiling housekeeper. "You remember how quiet and unspoiled our Spring has always been. Well, she needs to overcome her natural shyness."

Relieved that her aunt hadn't mentioned her humiliating experiences with men, Spring gazed at the two older women, praying this conversation would end as soon as possible.

Matilde nodded, her double chin quivering. "Yes, I remember. And Marco, ever since his father died, has stayed so serious. Working, saving, studying. He needs you in his life, Spring."

Matilde's words touched Spring's heart. Marco didn't need her. But if what Matilde said was true, Marco certainly needed to make a change. He did take life too seriously. He had overreacted to his sister helping Matilde. He didn't even want to take time to cater to three older ladies for a few meetings.

She would do what she could to help. If the ladies wanted to think she was "flirting" with him, well, it would provide them something fun to do, too. But she'd have to explain matters to Marco. She didn't

believe in manipulating a man, and Marco had always
been too proud, too intelligent to be "molded," anyway. But a life without fun wasn't healthy for Marco.

The next week Marco, this time in a black suit,
white shirt and black tie, towered over Spring sitting
on the country club veranda. Her nerves thrummed
inside her, but she kept her polite smile in place.

"Good afternoon."

Aunty, Eleanor and Verna Rae echoed her, beaming at him from their seats around the same table
they'd occupied last week.

Her pulse speeding up, Spring noted the way the
lines around Marco's mouth tightened even as he
smiled. *Please relax, Marco.* He sat down beside her.
Waves of tension radiated from him. *Why are you
wound so tightly, Marco? What is it deep inside you
that makes you try so hard?* She worked hard to reveal only a reserved mask. Marco, so close, drew her
attention and awakened her senses to everything
about him. The scent of his lime aftershave, his long
slender fingers, the way his ebony hair glistened in
the sunlight.

"Today we have to go over our list of sponsors,"
Verna Rae began, intruding on Spring's musing.

"What do your sponsors contribute?" Spring
asked, fighting the effect of Marco's nearness.

The three ladies turned their attention to her.
Eleanor replied, "Our sponsors contribute money for
advertising, dahling, and for the prizes we give the
winners."

Spring nodded. This kind of meeting was second nature to her. She held onto the familiar in spite of Marco's presence. "How many entries were there last year?"

Eleanor glanced at her notes. "Fifty-three."

"That many?" Spring gave a nod of approval. "Who were last year's sponsors?"

The meeting droned on.

Ring-ring, ring-ring. Marco reached for the cell phone at his belt.

At the sound, Spring felt her neck muscles tighten. The three other women paused to gaze at him with worried pouts.

After a brief phone exchange, he rose, looking relieved instead of concerned. "I've been called to the hospital. One of my patients has been brought in. My apologies." Then he looked pointedly at Spring. "Would you walk me to my car? I'd like to ask you a favor."

Feeling conspicuous, Spring stood up, wondering if the plan she'd come up with would fit the bill....

With a polite nod to the ladies at the table, he ushered her down the central hallway. His sleeve brushed against her bare arm. She tingled.

"Did you think of a way for me to get out of the committee gracefully?" He spoke close to her ear.

His warm breath against her skin sent pleasurable chills up her nape. Spring stepped outside into the dazzling sunshine. Gathering her courage, she said, "Why don't you take me to dinner tonight?"

"Dinner?" Marco looked puzzled. "What has dinner got to do with anything?"

"We need to go away somewhere and talk." *And my aunt and Matilde will think I'm coming out of my shell, so they won't humiliate us by "helping."*

Confusion in his expression gave way to understanding. "I see! When would you like me to pick you up?"

"Seven." *I don't think you do see, but…*

"Excellent." He slid behind the wheel of his car. "I really appreciate your helping with this. Thanks."

Trying to suppress an unexpected elation, Spring watched him drive down the boulevard lined with rosy azaleas. She realized she was playing with fire: spending time with Marco could endanger her concealment of her secret feelings for him. *You're going to learn how to have some fun, Marco—and fast—so this risky strategy I'm following ends before disaster occurs.*

But a smile played around the corners of her mouth as she walked back to the ladies on the veranda.

Three pairs of curious eyes gazed at her.

"Well?" Aunty prompted.

A grin Spring couldn't stop lifted the corners of her mouth. "He's picking me up for dinner at seven tonight."

"Hot dog!" Eleanor squealed. The three octogenarians performed an impromptu high-five times three.

Spring felt a little giddy. She sank down onto the chair. *It isn't a real date,* she reminded herself. But her heart refused to listen to her silly common sense. Dinner at seven with Marco!

Chapter Four

"**I** just know you've messed up." Doree's strident voice accosted Spring. She had picked up the beige front hall phone.

Spring frowned. "And hello to you, too. No, I haven't asked Aunt Geneva yet—"

"Why not?" Doree shouted.

"Doree, I won't let you abuse me over the phone. You think everything is easy about this, but it isn't." *Grow up, Doree.* "Asking about Mother's family is not easy."

Doree groaned. "You don't have all year. You only took a three-month leave of absence."

Did Doree really think she was delaying everything on purpose? "I am quite aware of the amount of time I have. I'll call you in a few days."

"Well, you had better!" Doree scolded and hung up.

How could her sister think Mother's health didn't

matter to her? For a few seconds, the urge to redial her younger sister and tell her to back off swept through Spring mightily, but she resisted it. Doree was very young and naturally brash. But Doree wasn't the one asking the question. So far, all Doree had done was crack the whip over her two sisters. Maybe Doree would feel differently if the shoe were on the other foot. *Dear Lord, help me ask soon.*

"Are you wearing those shoes?" Aunty asked in a disapproving tone, coming up the hall behind Spring.

Spring looked down at the bone low-heeled pumps she wore. "Yes, are they smudged on the back or something?" She turned one heel to glance at it.

"You need a higher heel. Come to my room."

High heels? Spring trailed after her aunt. "I don't like to wear high heels. They're uncomfortable—"

"Men love women in high heels." Aunty nudged Spring in front of her into the bedroom, then led her to the huge walk-in closet. "It's fortunate we wear the same shoe size."

Spring tried to think of a way to avoid her aunt's assistance. Aunty's shoes fit Spring in size, but not in age bracket. And did she really "fit" high heels? Spring doubted this.

"Let's pull out a few pairs I've saved." Aunty deftly pulled open a drawer from the back of her closet.

Looking over her aunt's shoulder, Spring glimpsed rows and rows of high heels in every color of the spectrum. Had Aunty saved every pair she'd ever owned? "I don't remember seeing you wear any of these."

"These are my favorites from the past. See this pair—my wedding shoes." Aunty displayed a pair of white silk pumps obviously made when Franklin Delano Roosevelt still slept in the White House.

Her wedding shoes! Spring reached for them. "Oh, Aunty! I—"

"No time for nostalgia now. Marco will arrive at any time. Here, try these—" Aunty put away her wedding shoes and brought out a pair of gold-colored sling-backs with three-inch heels.

Gaudy was the word that leaped to Spring's mind. "I don't think I've ever worn—"

"Try them." Aunty pushed them into her hands.

Feeling like some bizarre Cinderella, Spring obediently kicked off her comfortable pumps and slipped on the heels. Her feet looked like they belonged to someone else.

"Now walk up and down the room in front of my wall mirror," Aunty ordered.

Spring wanted to refuse, but stiffened her resolve. She did want Marco to see her as more than just an "old college acquaintance" this evening. Maybe golden slippers would jar him into reassessing her. Without glancing at the mirror, she walked back and forth across the large room. The height of the heels made her feel wobbly. They shortened her stride, too. In spite of these reactions, Spring tried to walk naturally.

Aunt Geneva studied her. "Ivory is a good color

for you. I like that sundress. It's a little long, but it skims your figure nicely.''

Spring didn't know what to say to this, so she gave no reply. Aunty had taught her all about fashion, but she'd never mentioned how to attract men with one's style.

''I think that jacket has to come off, though.''

Spring paused. ''I thought it might be a little cool this evening.''

''Then, carry it over your arm. And if you need it, be sure to ask Marco to put it around you. It's just the kind of intimate gesture that you should use to snag his interest.''

Spring closed her eyes, wondering if she was still in her right mind. *I don't do things like this.* But she obediently removed the matching linen jacket and laid it across her arm.

''Look at yourself as you walk.''

Spring glanced up and gave her aunt a quizzical look. ''What?''

''You need more sway to take full advantage of the high-heel effect,'' Aunty explained as she motioned with her hands.

''What's the high-heel effect?'' Spring stared at her.

''Look in the mirror.''

Spring obeyed. ''What am I looking for?''

Aunty rolled her eyes in mock dismay. ''Don't you see how it makes your legs look longer and how it tips you just a bit forward?''

Drawing close, Spring studied herself in the wall

mirror, turned sideways. She did appear a bit different. "You're right. I never knew!"

Aunty shook her head and muttered something Spring couldn't understand. "Dear, I wouldn't ask you to make these little changes, but you're trying to attract a man who ignores women, ignores a woman like *you*! You have to shake him out of this, this…fog he's in!" Aunty stepped back and scanned her niece.

Spring pursed her lips. "This just doesn't feel like me…."

"It's just a side of you we haven't let out before."

Sighing, Spring decided to let the changes Aunty had made stand. Marco seemed a true challenge for her to tackle with her first attempt at being… approachable.

"Anything else?" Spring propped one hand on her hip.

Drawing close, Aunty gave her a quick hug. "One more thing. Come over to my jewelry case."

Aunty's antique oak jewelry armoire stood three-feet high next to her vintage gilded vanity table. While Aunty sat, opening and closing drawers, she motioned Spring to settle on the adjacent chair. "Ah, this is just what we want." She held up a thin gold *Y* chain. "Dr. Da Palma needs a little direction, and this will keep his eyes on you." She slipped the gossamer chain over Spring's head and arranged it so that the two golden teardrop ends dangled above the sundress's *V* neckline.

Spring shivered as the chain settled onto her sensitive skin. *Oh, Lord, this just seems so artificial, so planned. I want Marco to notice me, just for me. Do I really need to make this effort? Is this just a silly crush I should have gotten over—*

Her aunt's musical doorbell rang.

Spring's heart leaped into her dry throat. She drew in a deep breath, then rose and picked up her jacket.

"This is it," Aunty murmured, beaming with anticipation. "I dare Dr. Da Palma to ignore you tonight!"

Spring nodded, feeling a bit queasy. But she didn't give in to the weakness. She marched down the hall toward the door.

"Slow down, dear!" Aunty urged in an undertone.

Spring slowed and tried to walk more femininely, or in a way Aunt Geneva would think looked more feminine. *I feel like a mannequin in a department store! This just isn't me, Lord!*

As Matilde opened the door for Marco, she beamed at Spring.

Spring looked up and caught Marco's expression. Framed by the doorway, wearing a dark suit, he looked handsome, but as uncomfortable as she felt.

A rush of excitement caught her by surprise. At last, she was going out with Marco. Never mind that she'd had to do the asking. To gain control, she inhaled, then said in a friendly tone, "Good evening, Marco. You're right on time."

"I have early rounds at seven tomorrow morning," he said with a straight face.

Matilde exhaled loudly, then scolded, "This is not the time to talk of work! You pick up a lovely *se-*

ñorita and you already tell her you will not take her out for long?'' She finished with a tart-sounding Spanish phrase.

Marco looked pained.

Matilde made him feel silly, just as her aunt was exasperating her.

Better get a move on! Picking up her handbag from the hall table, Spring stepped over the threshold past Marco. ''Don't wait up for me, Aunty.'' *Where had that come from? An old movie?*

She walked on, trying to remember to walk like…what? A movie star? Fashion model?

Marco hurried after her.

She reached his car first but waited for him. She tensed as he drew near.

''Is there something wrong with your lower back?'' Marco opened the car door for her. ''You're walking a little differently than usual.''

Spring groaned inside but gave him a bright smile. ''New shoes.''

''Maybe you should exchange them for ones with a different heel. Those don't look very comfortable.'' He slid into the car next to her.

Good grief. Was Marco even impervious to the ''high-heel effect''? ''I'll keep that in mind. Where are we going?''

''I don't know.'' He started the car and drove down the drive. ''Where would you like to go?''

Marco's lime aftershave filled the small space of the front seat. Spring's mind went blank. ''Anywhere is fine.''

"All right."

She tried to think of another topic, but nothing came to mind. Fortunately, Marco drove without asking further questions.

Ten minutes later, he led her into a modest Greek restaurant near the downtown section by the hospital. A middle-aged waitress with a thick accent seated them and handed them menus.

Spring held the menu and gazed around her at the unprepossessing restaurant—a counter, tables, booths and nondescript carpet and neutral colors. For *this,* she had scrutinized her whole Florida wardrobe and suffered three-inch heels?

"We can go somewhere else, if you like." Glancing over his menu at her, Marco looked unsure of himself.

"No, this is fine. Do you eat here often?"

"It's near the hospital."

"I see." Her flattened tone must have nicked him.

"I'm sorry it's not very special, but I know the food is good here," he said, sounding defensive.

"You misunderstood me. I love Greek food. I just thought..." How could she fault him? She'd forced him to take her out. But he'd brought her to the restaurant he ate at frequently because it was near the hospital and had good food. This proved true every worry Aunt Geneva and Matilde had. The man had no clue about dating! Even if Matilde hadn't already told them, Spring knew now that Marco didn't date much. He didn't even have a regular "date" place or two ready when needed.

"I thought of taking you to the country club, but then people might have thought we were actually dating."

Stung, Spring demanded, "Would that have ruined your reputation or mine?"

"What?" Marco eyed her with suspicion.

Spring bit her lower lip. The man was impossible. She'd seen an English comedy where the husband and wife were arguing in the kitchen and the wife had begun throwing the carrots she was peeling at the husband. Now Spring knew just how the woman had felt!

She eyed the basket of hard rolls on the table, but decided against tossing any at Marco. He'd probably have her rushed to the psych ward at the hospital across the way.

The morose waitress returned. Spring ordered the moussaka and Marco ordered the gyros dinner. The waitress walked away, and Spring and Marco just stared at one another.

"Have you given any thought to how I can gracefully get out of the garden show committee?" Marco picked out a roll as though trying to do something to cover his uneasiness.

Stalling, Spring scanned the other couples eating at the tables around them. How could Marco have brought her here for a cozy dinner? Most appeared to be medical employees or lone people who might have relatives at the hospital. No doubt the food here ranked above the hospital cafeteria's. She supposed she should be grateful Marco hadn't taken her there!

To Spring's left, however, sat a young couple in a booth. She could tell they were on a date. She studied the girl's posture. She was leaning forward with her elbows on the table, closer to her young man. Spring frowned. She'd been raised to never put her elbows on the table. But she needed to learn how to appear...available.

Spring gingerly set one elbow on the table and leaned forward a little.

"Well?" Marco insisted. "Have you thought of an out for me?"

Spring looked into his mahogany-brown eyes and was snared. She couldn't look away. *Oh, Marco, notice me. I can't help noticing you.*

"Is something wrong?"

Startled back to the present, she gave him a bright, persuasive smile. "No! I have some...information for you." She leaned closer to him.

"You make it sound like it's something I don't want to hear."

The girl to Spring's left giggled and leaned farther forward on the tabletop. Spring quickly looked away. *I'm not a teenager!*

She settled back against her seat, letting her hands drop to her lap. "You must promise not to repeat this, because they meant well."

"Who meant well and about what?"

"My aunt and her two friends are concerned that you work too hard and don't take any time for fun."

Marco stared at her, his lips parted in surprise.

Well, she certainly had his attention now. She

imagined leaning across the table and touching his lips with her fingertips. That unquestionably would be a signal of her interest in him—but they were in a Greek restaurant, not on lovers' lane. *Lord, I'm no good at this. Show me how to let him know I'd like to find out if we could be more than old college acquaintances.*

The waitress intruded silently, setting in front of them their Greek salads, fragrant of herbed oil-and-vinegar dressing, and their tall glasses of iced tea with generous lemon wedges. Then she left them.

Marco picked up his fork, but merely held it in his hand. "Fun? Are you trying to tell me the garden show meetings are being held for *my* amusement?"

Spring sighed. The girl to her left traced the rim of her soft drink glass and flirted with her eyes. Spring copied the tracing movement, but didn't flirt. She didn't feel up to it now.

"Marco, the ladies have watched you grow up. They are very proud of your success, happy they were able to be of help to you. But their interest in you doesn't stop with your becoming their doctor." *Help me, Lord. Please don't let this sound lame.* "They want to see you happy and…having fun." She left out *happily married,* for obvious reasons.

He stared at her.

She traced the rim of her iced tea glass, then took a sip of lemon tea to moisten her dry mouth. The teenage girl gave a provocative giggle. *Who had taught her how to do that?*

"You have got to be kidding." He looked at her with desperate eyes.

"I'm not kidding."

"Are you sure this is…why I'm on that committee?"

She nodded.

He put down his fork. "Why do they care?"

She glanced again into his dark eyes. She knew many men didn't easily comprehend human relationships. Father did, but his job had included counseling so he'd studied human psychology and listened to Mother.

"Because they are good people. They like you."

"But I worked as a caddie at the club. I washed dishes there. I was just a young immigrant boy who qualified for scholarships…"

She straightened. Did he believe that nonsense? Is that how he saw himself? "So you were a caddie. What does that matter? Don't you realize that most of the Golden Sands members are self-made men and women? They succeeded and they wanted you to succeed, too. What's so mysterious about that?"

His intense gaze made her face warm with a blush. "My aunt Geneva was the daughter of a carpenter. She and her husband served in World War II. After the war, her husband took the risk of becoming a contractor and made his money in the postwar building boom. Eleanor is the daughter of immigrants from Russia, and Verna Rae's family were farmers. None of them was born with a silver spoon in her mouth."

Marco turned this new idea over in his mind. The

people at the country club viewed him as...what? Something like a son, a protégé? Was that possible? "I always felt..." He looked to Spring. "I never thought of it that way before."

She nodded. A gold chain glimmered around her ivory neck. Something was different about Spring tonight. Her serenity didn't appear quite as complete as usual. Why wasn't a beautiful and elegant woman like her married by now?

"But what has that and the garden show meetings got to do with having fun?"

She smiled, though her mouth looked stiff, disapproving. "They want you to take time to enjoy your success." She folded her hands like a bridge over her salad. "Aunty says the older one gets, the more one treasures the *intangibles* of life. They won their success with hard work, but they know what success costs. I think the three ladies want you to learn earlier than their own husbands did that all of us should take time—"

"To smell the roses?" he finished for her, his tone terse.

Spring gazed back at him with a serious expression, then tensed, "Well, if you help with the garden show, you certainly will be in a position to do that." She took a bite of a tomato wedge, and eyed him while she chewed.

He squirmed under her regard. "So that means I can't just resign from the committee?"

She took another sip of iced tea. "I have an alternative to suggest."

Her every move was so graceful, it was hard for him to look away. "What?"

"You need to show that you're taking time to have some fun. What hobbies do you have?"

Forking up some of the salad, he considered her question. Spring's beauty distracted him. Swallowing, he shook his head. "No hobbies."

Spring made a face at him. "You caddied. Did you ever play golf?"

He shook his head. "No time."

She sighed loudly. "There's another matter I haven't mentioned, but which the ladies are also concerned about."

"About me?"

"Yes." She skewered a Kalamata olive and popped it into her mouth.

His mouth went dry. "I'm afraid to ask."

She lifted her eyebrows.

"All right." He cleared his throat. "I'll bite. What else am I neglecting?"

"You're not dating."

After dinner, Marco walked with Spring to the parking lot and opened her car door for her.

"It's a bit chilly. Help me with my jacket?" Looking over her shoulder, she handed it to him.

He took it and helped her slide her slender arms into the sleeves. When he pulled it up around her neck, she reached up to adjust the collar and her fingers brushed his. Warmth rushed through him.

She slid inside the car. "Thanks."

Reeling from his reaction to her, he nodded, then walked around and let himself into the driver's seat. All that Spring had said to him seemed to parade in his mind like announcements on one of those lighted marquees you saw on TV: *THE GOLDEN SANDS LADIES THINK YOU WORK TOO MUCH... THEY'VE WATCHED YOU GROW UP AND ARE PROUD OF YOU....THEY THINK YOU SHOULD BE DATING....*

The messages boggled his mind. Spring's nearness had breached his carefully tended defenses, sending disconcerting sensations through him.

"Will you think over my suggestion?" Spring asked.

He tried to focus on her words. "You mean, that I need a hobby?"

"Yes."

"Do you think it will get me off the committee?" He still had a hard time believing what she'd explained.

"If they see that you're having fun—"

"With you?" This suggestion was the most dangerous to his equilibrium. Spring affected him too much. He'd mapped out his life. A woman like her would never be within his reach.

"Well, is there someone else you'd prefer?" She glanced at him in the low light.

Someone else? Anyone else! He kept emotion out of his voice. "No, but no one would believe that you'd be interested in dating someone like me—"

"Someone like you," Spring snapped. "What's wrong with you?"

Her words stung him. "After all you said at dinner, if I didn't know you better, didn't know you are as truthful as the day is long, I'd think you were nuts!"

"If you think that I'm somehow beyond you, you *are* nuts. You seemed to have a really off-kilter way of looking at yourself, Golden Sands and me."

She said he was "nuts." Spring had always spoken so formally. He had to bring her to her senses. She had to face reality. "At the university, you pledged at one of the most exclusive sororities. You weren't on scholarship and working—"

"You've got it all wrong, Marco. My father is a pastor of a small church in Wisconsin. We aren't a wealthy family." Her words surged over him. "Aunt Geneva paid my way through college and insisted I pledge a sorority. She also helped both my sisters with their educations. But since I decided to go to school here, Aunt Geneva helped me more. I told you that you have some funny ideas about my family, about me."

"Maybe I do." *But I doubt it. Your father wouldn't welcome me, an Hispanic immigrant, with open arms. Just because I'm a doctor now doesn't change who I am and who you are. No matter what you say.* That point had been driven home to him on more than one occasion in college.

He pulled up to Mrs. Dorfman's front door.

Spring said in a stiff tone, "Don't get out. I'll see

myself to the door. You said you have an early morning.''

She sounded *muy enojado*, very upset. Why? ''Spring, I—''

With a wave to Marco, Spring walked to the door and into the house. The man was impossible! Dense! This plan would never work! One of her high heels pinched her toes, but she didn't slow. She closed the door behind her.

The house was only dimly lit, but this didn't fool her. She stifled her frustration. She couldn't dash Matilde's and Aunty's hopes. ''Aunt Geneva?''

''We're in your aunt's room,'' Matilde called out. ''Come. We've been waiting!''

Spring walked down the hallway toward the light. The sound from the TV suddenly cut off.

Matilde in a bright turquoise robe met her at the door. ''Where did he take you?''

Exhausted from an evening of trying to be different, more desirable than usual, Spring walked past Matilde over to the chair beside Aunty's chaise longue. She collapsed onto it.

Aunty sat up. Her housekeeper hurried after her and perched on the end of the chaise.

Shrugging out of her jacket, Spring sighed. ''He took me to a Greek restaurant near the hospital.''

''Not to the country club?'' Aunty raised her eyebrows.

''Not to the Riviera Restaurant on the Boulevard?'' Matilde complained, crestfallen.

"I don't think he considered it a real date, so he just took me to a restaurant he was used to."

Matilde grimaced and shook her head. "The man is *loco*. A beautiful *señorita* like you, he takes to a plain restaurant!"

Aunty studied her intensely. "Do you think you made any progress with him?"

Spring sighed and slipped off the heels. "He's going to be a hard nut to crack. But I think I've got him thinking."

"Thinking? About what?" Matilde demanded.

"About there being more to life than work."

"Well—" Aunty drew in a long breath "—that's a start."

"I'll pray tonight for you, *querida*." Rising, Matilde patted Spring's cheek. "Marco isn't stupid, but you have much to teach him."

Spring nodded. When Matilde closed the door behind her, Spring looked to her great-aunt. "Are you too tired to talk?"

"What is it?"

Spring leaned back against the chair and closed her eyes for a moment, drained but keyed up. "I don't have the energy to pose this gracefully. I've been trying to ask you a very important question since I arrived here over a week ago. The right time never seems to come—"

"What is it?"

"Was your childhood friend, Connie Wilson, my mother's biological parent?"

Chapter Five

Aunt Geneva stared at Spring, openmouthed.

Her heart suddenly thudding, Spring waited for several moments, then she prompted, "Aunty, will you tell me?"

"What…why?" Aunty shook her head. "How?"

"My sisters and I are afraid that Mother might come out of remission—"

"But she's been fine! Why are you worrying?"

"She is now, but she's still tested every three months. Remission isn't the same as cured. Recurrence is always possible."

Aunty looked shocked, unhappy.

Spring reached for her aunt's hand. "We want to be prepared. Not one of us girls was a bone marrow match."

"I was tested, too." Aunty squeezed Spring's hand but looked down.

"Mother didn't tell us that you were tested."

"Of course I was."

Spring leaned closer. "And you didn't match, either?"

Her aunt shook her head as though in pain. "We're not blood relatives, after all. There was only the slimmest possibility of a match."

"Then, you know how helpless we felt." Releasing her aunt, Spring leaned back, feeling her own deep weariness. "We just can't let it drop. If at all possible, we want to locate Mother's natural parents—"

"No!"

"Why are you so adamant?" Spring observed her aunt closely for her reaction. "Why won't you tell me about Connie Wilson?"

Her aunt seemed stricken. "Who is Connie Wilson? Who gave you that name?"

"You did."

Aunty's mouth fell open again. "I never did."

Pursing her lips, Spring nodded. "You did. You showed me a photograph of you and grandmother and a friend—"

"When?" Aunty snapped. "I don't remember that."

Spring went on gently, "I remembered your friend's name, Connie Wilson."

"It's a very common name. I might have had a friend with that name." Aunty stared at her hands.

"But you acted very upset that you'd showed it to me. I couldn't figure out at the time why you were so quick to regret that I saw that photograph of the three of you."

"I don't remember it at all. Besides, who told you a Connie Wilson was Ethel's mother?"

"Your sister—my grandmother—told Father on her deathbed."

Aunty frowned and looked as though she was struggling against tears. "It's not what you think—and you're asking me about events that happened over fifty years ago."

"It doesn't matter how long ago Mother was born and adopted. My sisters and I have decided we must find her natural parents."

"I can't believe that Ethel has agreed to this—"

"She hasn't." Spring rested her head back against the chair.

"You're going against her wishes, behind her back?" Aunty turned pink with agitation.

Spring nodded. "My sisters and I can't stand the thought that she might need a donor and might die because none can be found in time."

"But even if you located— They might not agree to be tested."

"That's right, but at least we'll have done all we can do to help Mother. We won't contact them, just locate them. We'd be ready if her remission ends. Now will you tell me about Connie Wilson?"

Aunt Geneva shook her head. "I'm sorry, dear. You know how much I love your mother. I only had one sister. We were both childless, and she only adopted one child, your mother. There's much about this you don't know—and you're asking me to break a promise I made to my sister fifty years ago. I can't do so without a lot of thought and prayer."

"That's what Father said when we asked him for help, but surely you can understand how difficult this is for my sisters and me."

Spring waited, silently praying for God's will.

Aunty moved her hands in a nervous gesture, then touched her temple as though it pained her. "I'm very tired—"

Accepting this dismissal, Spring rose, kissed her aunt's lined cheek and paused. "Do you know how much I love you?"

With a wan smile, Aunty patted her face. "I love you, too, my dear. Now go to bed. It's been a long day and night."

Spring nodded, and dragged her tired body down the hall to her room. She undressed beside her bed, then donned her pink pajamas and slipped between the crisp sheets. The word *exhaustion* didn't come close to describing how tired she felt. Her body and mind ached with fatigue. She hated the shock she'd just given her dear aunt. *Lord, bless her, my family. Bless Marco and help me know what I'm to do about Mother and about loving him.*

As soon as Spring was fully awake the next morning, she dialed her bedside phone. When the ringing stopped and a familiar voice answered, she said impetuously, "Hannah, I'm so glad I got you! I don't know what I would have done if you hadn't picked up."

"Spring, you sound upset."

"I am. Last night I asked Aunt Geneva about Connie Wilson—"

"What did she say?" Hannah's voice was eager.

"She bluffed her way through it."

"What do you mean?"

"I dropped the name Connie Wilson on her, and she tried to deny any knowledge without—"

"—actually denying it," Hannah finished. "What are your plans?"

"I'll wait her out. Keep praying."

"I will."

Spring needed help on another front: handling Doree. "And do me a favor. You remember how it feels to be on the front line—"

"I do. Don't worry. I'll relay this to Doree."

"And—"

"And I'll threaten her with dismemberment if she calls to bother you!"

Spring sighed. "I love you, sweet sister."

"Ditto."

"How's Guthrie?"

"I love him so much, my teeth ache!"

Spring laughed out loud and said goodbye. *Lucky Hannah!* She'd found her true love on a church roof.

Wearing a white dress with a *V* neck and puffed sleeves, Paloma sat in the wicker chair in Aunt Geneva's garden. Spring picked up her pastels and began to sketch Paloma's face and form.

"Your choice of dress is excellent," Spring murmured.

"I bought it for her." Matilde sat beside Aunt Geneva and behind Spring. Paloma had spent most of this Saturday helping Matilde clean cupboards in the kitchen and pantry. "I want this portrait to be a surprise for Santos and Anita."

"I'll do my very best," Spring promised. "I hope your parents will be pleased."

Paloma scowled. "Nothing pleases my father."

"*Querida,*" Matilde soothed, "he just wants what's best for your future."

"I got a *B-* on a math test, and he acts like it's the end of the world! I'm grounded for a whole week!"

That did seem a bit strong. On the paper, Spring outlined Paloma's shoulders and began carefully sketching in her arms. "The week will be over before you know it," Spring said encouragingly.

Matilde nodded. "You will do better on the next test, and everything will be fine."

Spring smiled at Paloma. "I need you to relax. I know this can be tiring, but you'll do fine."

The young girl relaxed her shoulders and lifted a subdued but smiling face to Spring.

"Perhaps your brother could talk to your father?" Aunt Geneva suggested.

"My half-brother never talks to my father. My father talks, but Marco never says anything but *sí, no, gracias* and *de nada.*"

"Marco will come around someday," Matilde predicted placidly.

Marco is definitely a stubborn man, Spring agreed silently. I wonder why he won't talk to his stepfather?

Three days later, Marco looked as if he were close to being in a coma. On the Golden Sands veranda, the garden show committee was in the midst of its third meeting. Spring tried to look interested, or at least awake. How could she be so bored, yet keyed up at the same time?

Aunty asked, "Well, what is your decision?"

"I don't know," Eleanor exclaimed. "What do you think, Verna Rae?"

Spring couldn't even remember what they were trying to decide. Too many other thoughts kept popping up and distracting her.

Aunty had turned down another retirement home yesterday—the fourth one. *Doesn't Aunty want to move? Did she ask me down to help her or was it just a ruse to get me here for longer than one week? Does she need me more now that she is approaching ninety?* The thought wasn't a new one. She'd always known she'd move back when Aunty needed her. Had that time—?

"Maybe we should ask our male colleague?" Verna Rae drawled. "What do you think, Doctor? Should we take out an ad in the *Suncoaster?*"

Marco's eyes had glazed over. "What?"

Spring couldn't help him now. She'd offered him a way out, but evidently he preferred sitting here through another interminable meeting to trying the alternative. This fact did nothing for her ego. She had to be rock bottom on his list.

Discouraged, she slouched against the back of her chair. Had he counted on his phone rescuing him this time, too?

Trying to ignore Marco was maddening. Because of temperatures in the humid eighties, he'd shed his suit jacket and tie. Didn't the man own anything but suits? His white shirt, unbuttoned at the top, revealed a *V* of strong, tanned neck. The breeze sent tantalizing hints of his lime scent. How could he snare her notice without even trying—especially when she'd tried to catch his and failed miserably?

Spring realized her low spirits had come from so many things, including her mother's illness and her aunt's refusal to tell her about Connie Wilson. But how could she not take Marco's attendance at the garden show meeting as a sign that he'd rather do *anything* than spend time with her? This reflection lodged in her throat like a rock.

All three of the ladies gazed at Marco.

He stared back at them.

He doesn't have a clue. Spring bridled.

"Why don't we take a vote?" he suggested.

Spring wanted to unmask his inattention and ask, *On what, Marco?* But she shouldn't embarrass him— even if he did find her unappealing.

The vote on buying the ad in the *Suncoaster* passed with unanimous approval, after Marco hesitantly raised his hand to make it so. And the meeting rumbled to an end.

As they all rose to depart, Marco cleared his throat. "Ladies, I'm sorry but I'm going to have to resign from the committee."

Spring held her breath. He'd refused her suggestions. What excuse would he give?

"I'm going to take Spring up on her offer to teach me how to play golf. I've been invited to participate in a March golf tournament, a fund-raiser for our hospital, and I need to prepare for it."

The three ladies beamed at him. Spring felt her lips part in surprise. She was just an amateur golfer herself! Still, a thrill shuddered through her. She tried to ignore it, but a smile lit her face and sparked a rosy glow deep inside her.

"Are you sure you haven't played golf before?" A few days later, Spring stood beside Marco at the club's driving range under a brilliant blue sky. She had dressed with care in white shorts and a blue, cotton-knit top. She had some concern about her appearance today, since Matilde had contributed her bit to Spring's new look. Saying Spring needed to do something more with her hair, Matilde had swept up one side of it with a tortoise-shell clip. A sheaf of blond hair rose over her ear and cascaded temptingly to her shoulder—at least, that's what Aunty had said. "You were a groundskeeper. You must know some golf."

"I know which club to use for which kind of shot. I know how to score. I know some other odds and ends."

His lack of enthusiasm could have been cut with a knife. Spring found this admission fit the peculiar attitude he had about himself and his relation to the country club that he'd revealed on their "date."

"But you never played?"

"I never had a set of clubs." He shrugged, looking away.

So he hadn't had clubs. And had he wanted to play, but feared jeering from the caddies?

Spring gazed at the green lawn in front of them. "Well, you do now—"

"Your aunt didn't need to give me her late husband's gear."

Spring swung her hair back over her shoulder. "It was just gathering dust. He was about your height, so we can use them to get started. You're just borrowing them until you have time to purchase your own—"

"I don't know that I intend to take this up—"

"My point exactly," she cut in. "Now, do you know how to take a proper stance when you address the ball?"

He said in a grim voice, "I know I have to stand in line with the hole and at right angles to the ball."

She ignored his tone and fidgeted with the gold locket on her neck. When she realized what she was doing, she dropped her nervous hand to her side. "Good. Set your tee and let's see your stance." She stepped back. *You specified golf lessons and you're going to get golf lessons!*

Without comment, Marco bent to set his tee and

ball. He selected the one wood from the bag and took his place beside the tee.

Spring eyed him critically, trying to ignore how handsome he looked in navy slacks and crisp white shirt with his cuffs rolled back—though it was not really golf garb. "Stand straight with your shoulders back, head up and arms at your sides."

Marco obeyed.

Her insides stuttered like a damaged CD, but she went on in a calm voice. "Keeping your back and legs straight, push your bottom out, bring your head over the ball."

Marco grunted but followed her instructions.

"Relax your knees." Giving Marco, a man who emanated intelligence and competence, simple directions struck Spring's funny bone. She suppressed a grin.

"Okay, what next?"

Spring had heard men sound happier when getting a parking ticket, but she said calmly, "Let your arms swing freely."

As instructed, he swung his arms—and grumbled more.

"You are now in address position. Now here's your club." She glimpsed an older man who stood a few feet away, watching them. Amusement lit his face. No doubt triggered by a *woman* trying to teach a *man* how to play golf.

Spring tried not to make eye contact with the stranger. She wasn't in the mood for any humorous comments about her teaching Marco. And this man looked like the kind of duffer who had a store of jokes he wished to share. Normally she'd indulge him, but Marco presented enough of a challenge to her patience already.

"Now let's see your grip." Spring motioned toward Marco.

He took the club and placed his hands around it, just so.

To view the grip from all angles, she bent and nudged his wrist slightly. She caught herself just before she slid her hand up the taut, smooth sinew of his arm. She turned her head and bumped noses with him. "Sorry." She blushed.

She cleared her throat. "Good. You must have learned the Vardon grip from watching others. It's the most successful—"

"Can I hit the ball now?" Marco asked in a voice that announced he was clutching the frayed ends of his patience.

Spring suppressed a sigh. She hadn't thought Marco would enjoy being taught by a woman. Marco was Latin, after all. Was this a token of his machismo?

"Go right ahead."

He swung and connected with the ball, which flew across the driving range.

"Not bad. You'll be ready for that golf fund-raiser before you know it." She glanced up at him, a thought occurring to her. "There really is a tournament, isn't there?"

He nodded. "I didn't enter it the past two years,

didn't have time." He grimaced. "I can't believe we're here really doing this."

His complaint cut her. "What's the big deal?" Was passing an hour or two with her such torture? "So you spend a couple of hours a week swinging a club and walking in the sunshine—all to prepare for a good cause. Is that an unhealthy way to spend your time, Doctor?"

"No, but I have—"

"Yes, I know you're a *very busy man.*" She shook her head at him. "But even the busiest man needs regular relaxation and exercise. I'm sure you've said that to a patient or two, haven't you?"

His expression told her that she'd "got" him. Without showing any visible satisfaction, she continued, "Now let's try that again."

Ring-ring. Ring-ring. Marco reached for his cell phone. "Hello."

For one moment, Spring glanced at the white, puffy clouds overhead. Had Marco prearranged a call just to get away? But she watched Marco's face draw down into serious lines.

"Yes, I'll come right away. Of course." His tone was laced with concern.

She watched him close the phone.

"I'm sorry I have to leave."

She took a step closer.

"Something's come up. I have to go."

She scanned his face. "You're looking really upset."

"It's nothing." He turned away to slide the shaft of his wood back into the golf bag.

She frowned. Should she press him? If he didn't look so apprehensive, she might guess that he'd grab at any straw to shorten their lesson. But his anxiety felt real.

Her natural inclination was to accept his evasive explanation, but she was trying to break out of her shell and into this man's life. She stood straighter.

"You're not being frank with me. What is it?"

Chapter Six

Marco stared at Spring. The question didn't sound like her at all. "I don't have time—"

"Fine. Let's go."

Did she sound disappointed? Why? Then another thought hit him. "I forgot that I drove you here," he apologized.

"No problem. I'll call a cab."

Her long tawny legs distracting him, he tried to figure out what she really meant. She'd told him she wanted to know why he was leaving, then said she'd just call a cab.

"I should take you home."

"Taking a cab is not a problem."

But it was to him—and though he didn't understand why, he just couldn't leave Spring here. This irritated him. He lifted the golf bag to his shoulder. Careful not to glance at her, he reached for Spring's golf bag, a wheeled version, to push it to the car for her. "I need to stop at the high school first."

"Did something happen to your sister?"

"Why would you ask that?" he asked in a sharper tone than he'd intended.

"I'm sorry, I just thought she might be ill…"

Why did this have to happen now? He'd been handling being close to Spring. He'd kept his mind on golf, ignoring her golden beauty. Pausing for a moment, he ran one hand, then the other, through his dark hair.

"It is about my sister."

She gazed at him as though waiting for him to say more, but his concern made him mute.

"Maybe I could be of help?" She looked up at him.

He directed his gaze skyward, trying to achieve perspective. *I'm making a mountain out of a molehill. It's just a high school scrape.* "Okay. The school called my stepfather, but he couldn't leave work right now. He's dealing with an emergency plumbing job and can't get away. My mother can't be reached."

"Is Paloma ill?"

He frowned. *I wish.* "I have to go to school to talk to the vice-principal. She's been suspended—"

"Paloma? I can't believe it. She's such a sweet girl. Would you like me to come along?"

Thrown by her offer, he started walking toward the parking lot. He couldn't deny that what she'd suggested appealed to him. Paloma, in trouble at school?

What could she possibly have done? "Would you…come along?"

"Of course, I will. Paloma must feel awful."

He snorted. "She's going to feel worse when my stepfather gets home." Maybe that's why he didn't feel comfortable going to get his sister. Paloma, now a teenager, had become a puzzle to him.

"We'd better get going," Spring urged. "Paloma needs us."

After a quick drive across town, Marco pushed open the heavy school door for Spring. Inside, the voice of a teacher explaining an algebraic equation drifted from the open door of a classroom. Marco hadn't been to the high school since he graduated. The dusty hallways lined with gray lockers brought back memories, feelings he'd totally forgotten. He hadn't liked them then; he didn't like remembering them now: uncertainty about himself, his ability to be good enough to achieve his goals and an edgy distance from those around him.

Each step gave him a bit more sympathy for his little sister. Did she have any of the same feelings? But she'd been born here. She'd never been a stranger in this country the way he had been.

A shrill bell stunned him, and a roar of voices and pounding of feet exploded in the hallway. The vice-principal's office loomed at the end of the hall. The crush of students bustled around them. Marco drew closer to Spring. He didn't like the way some of the teenage males were gawking at her. He ushered her to the door.

Inside the office, the secretary behind the counter sat at her desk, talking on the phone. A line of dejected students slouched on a row of rigid plastic chairs along the wall. Paloma looked out of place among them. She glanced up and froze.

Spring walked directly over to her and leaned down to murmur in her ear. Spring sparkled in the drab setting like a diamond on faded cloth. He'd had the same feeling when he'd taken her to dinner. His life didn't seem to have the proper "settings" for someone like Spring.

Waiting for the secretary to get off the phone, Marco controlled his frustration while wondering what Spring was saying to his sister. What had Paloma done to get herself suspended?

The secretary hung up and looked to him. "You are?"

"I'm Paloma's brother, Dr. Da Palma."

The secretary glanced over to his sister. "Doctor, please come into the office. The vice-principal will talk to you now."

Marco looked at Spring. She patted Paloma's shoulder, then left her to accompany him. He let her precede him inside.

The gray-haired vice-principal jumped up and came around his desk to shake Marco's and Spring's hands, then seated her in a chair in front of his desk.

Marco didn't like the way the other man's eyes lingered on Spring, especially her legs. Marco made the introductions and sat down.

"What has my sister done?"

The man's gaze still centered on Spring, he began, "She's never been in trouble—"

"I know that," Marco said. "What has she done?"

The vice-principal stared at him. "She talked back to a teacher rudely, but what earned her a suspension was refusing to come to my office when told to do so."

"That doesn't sound like Paloma." Spring leaned toward the desk, her golden hair falling forward on one side. "I know she was upset about a test grade. Did this happen in math class?"

Distracted by the picture Spring presented, Marco forced himself to follow the exchange.

"Yes, yes." The vice-principal nodded. "That sounds like it might be what motivated this incident, but—"

"Low test score or no, Paloma knows she's supposed to obey her teachers." Marco glared at him. The man was ogling Spring. One thing Marco did know about Spring: she didn't like men drooling over her.

As though he realized what Marco was thinking, the man drew himself up and faced Marco. "That's why she's been suspended for one day. She won't be allowed back in school until Friday."

"Will she be allowed to make up work she's missed?" Spring asked.

"Yes, of course."

"Anything else?" Marco stood, ending the meeting.

The vice-principal rose, too. "No. Thank you for coming down. Normally, I wouldn't send a student home with anyone but a parent, but Paloma's father has given permission for me to release Paloma to you.''

Relieved to get Spring away, Marco nodded and led her from the office. At the secretary's motion, Paloma jumped up and joined Spring and him.

After the three of them had stopped at Paloma's crowded locker to get her things, they walked out the school doors into the bright winter sunshine. Marco drew in fresh, chalk-free air.

''What a big deal,'' Paloma grumbled.

''Your father better never hear you say that!'' Marco snapped. ''You'll be grounded for the rest of your life.''

''I will, anyway!'' Paloma yanked open Marco's car door and heaved her heavy schoolbag into the back seat. ''A one-day suspension! That teacher just has it in for me!''

Chagrined by his sister's tantrum, Marco opened his mouth, but before he could speak—

Spring opened her arms. ''Come here, Paloma.''

His sister hesitated, then let Spring enfold her. Paloma began to cry.

He observed Spring's strategy with some surprise. But the contrasting picture of the two of them, one fair and one dark, caught his attention. The urge to put his arms around both of them tugged at his control. He'd always thought Paloma pretty, but seeing her standing next to Spring made him realize how close his sister was to becoming a young woman. It also made him grateful to Spring. She seemed to know exactly what to say.

Spring held his sister and murmured words close to Paloma's ear that Marco couldn't hear. After a few moments, Spring brushed back the dark brown waves around his sister's face. "Now, no more angry words. You made a mistake. You'll make it right and it won't happen again."

"But you don't know my father—"

"Your father loves you and wants what is best for you." Spring placed one of her hands on each side of Paloma's face. "This too shall pass." She smiled. "That's my mother's old saying and it's a true one. Now slide into the back, and we'll drive you home."

Spring's words indebted Marco to her.

Though tears glistened on her face, Paloma obeyed, and Marco opened Spring's door so she could get into the passenger seat. He got in himself and drove away pondering the openhearted way Spring had reached out to Paloma. Evidently he'd made the right decision in bringing Spring along. Her gentle hug had certainly changed his sister's attitude. Personally, he'd felt more like shaking Paloma than hugging her.

His sister's suspension had caught him by surprise. He tried not to think how upset his stepfather would be. Santos wasn't a harsh man, but he was a strict father and he expected a lot from his only daughter.

Marco glanced sideways at Spring. Now he could take Spring back to her world, where she belonged. "I'll drop you at your aunt's home first."

"If that's what you want. I'm fine either way." She rested her slender arm along the open window. Fine freckles like gold dusted its length.

Why did he always have to notice things like that about her? He turned right, heading for Highway 19, which would take them to Mrs. Dorfman's Gulf shore home. His cell phone rang.

He took it from his pocket, lifted it to his ear. "Hello." His mother's voice answered him. "Your car? Where are you, Mother?" With a sinking sensation, he listened to her tangled explanation. "The school—" Pause. "I'll come right away. No, I insist. The corner of Bayshore and Main."

"I'm sorry, Spring," he apologized, frustration stinging him. "I've got to—"

Spring cut in. "Your mother is waiting at the corner of Bayshore and Main. Did she have car trouble?"

He nodded.

"That's fine. I told you, I'm in no hurry." She lifted her blond hair from her neck. "The day's getting warm."

Ignoring as best he could the lovely pose she presented, he turned left at a green light and headed toward the older section of Gulfview, the one he'd left behind at fourteen when his mother had married Santos.

"I don't like her waiting alone down there—"

"Someone from the halfway house is probably with her," Paloma said. "They take good care of her, or Dad wouldn't let her go."

Marco didn't answer, but drove on. To have Spring beside him and not show his awareness of her was becoming an increasing trial. What a day! First his sister, now his mother's car problems—all the while, Spring beside him, forcing him to deal with the attraction to her he'd thought he conquered.

As soon as he picked up his mother, he'd drop Spring off and head to the hospital. He was glad he didn't have anything serious to deal with this afternoon. *I just need to call and check on Mr. Gardner.*

"Does your mother work at the halfway house?" With both hands, Spring pulled her abundant hair back into a ponytail.

Though aggravated with himself, Marco admired her slender, pale neck.

"Yeah, she volunteers there to teach the women how to sew their own clothes." Paloma obviously had found some bubble gum. Marco smelled the distinctive sweet aroma. A bubble popped behind him.

"What kind of halfway house is it?" Spring dropped her hair and shook her head, letting her fine golden hair settle around her shoulders.

"It's for recovering drug offenders," Marco said, hoping that would put an end to this line of conversation. Why did women always want to know all the details?

Spring said, "I've never been able to accomplish more than just mending. My mother and my sister Doree, though, sew beautifully."

He lifted an eyebrow. *Her mother sews? Why?* Spring always wore the very best—anyone could see that.

Paloma popped another bubble. "You've got a sister?"

"I have two sisters, Hannah and Doree," Spring replied.

"Those are great names. Where'd they get them?" Paloma asked.

"We were all named for women in my father's family."

"Gee, that's how I got stuck with my name."

"There's nothing wrong with your name," Marco said in a low voice.

Paloma began, "Oh, yeah—"

Spring cut in smoothly. "It was my mother's idea. She was fascinated by my father's family Bible that listed all the deaths and births for five generations. She never liked her name—"

"What's her name?" his sister interrupted.

"Ethel."

"That's worse than Paloma!"

Marco let out a slow breath. *All this about a name.*

Spring opened her purse and pulled out a tiny jar. "Paloma's a lovely name. It means 'dove,' doesn't it?"

"Yeah, but what's so great about being named for a bird?"

Spring dipped her little finger into the jar, then applied the finger to her soft-looking lips. "The dove is a special bird. When Christ was baptized by John, the Spirit of God came down from heaven in the form of a dove and it rested on Jesus. And when Noah wanted to know if the waters were receding, he sent out a dove to fly over the land. The dove is a symbol of God's presence. It's a beautiful name."

"Gee, nobody ever told me about it that way. My dad says there has been a Paloma in his family every generation since before America was a country."

Out of the corner of his eye, Marco noticed that whatever Spring had applied to them, her lips looked dewy, thoroughly kissable….

"How wonderful." Spring licked her lips, then pressed them together.

"What does Doree mean?" Paloma watched Spring as though memorizing her every move.

"It means 'golden one.'" Spring capped the tiny jar and slipped it back into her bag. "My other sister is Hannah, 'graceful one.' Both were named for great-grandmothers."

Marco had driven them to what people had twenty years ago called Spanish Town, before political correctness had come in vogue. It was the old downtown of the original city. In spite of urban renewal attempts, a few storefronts remained boarded up.

Spring pointed to a Mexican restaurant ahead. "That looks like a good place to eat."

"That's Mamacita's," Paloma enthused. "It's great! They have the best tacos in town."

Glancing over her shoulder, Spring grinned at the girl. "You sound hungry."

"I am. I missed lunch."

"Well, so did we." Spring touched Marco's arm.

He tightened his resistance to her, but she was sitting so near. She had been calm in the face of his sister's ill temper and now her slender form was so at ease next to him. She casually lifted her hair off her nape with a flip of her wrist. All too aware of her movement, he made himself stare at the road ahead. He was melting inside, and it wasn't because of the temperature.

Spring suggested, "After we pick up your mother, why don't we stop at Mamacita's for lunch?"

"Mamacita's?" Marco echoed. Mamacita's was a great restaurant, but he couldn't imagine Spring enjoying a meal there. He'd been ashamed he'd made the blunder of taking her to the Greek restaurant the other night. He should have thought of someplace special to take her. But he hadn't wanted her to think he assumed it was a date, and in the end, she'd probably concluded he didn't know that she deserved better. Men didn't take a beauty like Spring to just anyplace!

Spring grinned at him. "I'm definitely in the mood for Mexican today."

Her grin made him forget his irritation, but—

Paloma gave a hoot of agreement.

Fighting the effect of Spring's glowing face, Marco shook his head. "That isn't the kind of place you'd like to eat lunch."

"Why not?" Paloma demanded. "Mamacita's is great. They make their own tortillas and their *sopaipillas* are to die for!"

"Then, Mamacita's is *definitely* my kind of place." Spring angled herself on the seat so she faced him— turning her loveliness on him full force.

Marco shored up his resolve, but her effect on him couldn't be blunted.

At the start of the day, he'd been irritated even to have to spend the morning learning to hit a little ball around to please the garden committee ladies. The brief golf lesson had been all the time in Spring's presence he'd been prepared to handle.

Suffering the temptingly beautiful woman beside him as the day progressed had become a test he didn't want to continue. And he certainly didn't want to involve her in his family problems. Irritation simmered in his stomach. Nothing was going as he'd planned!

He spotted his mother in the block ahead, right in front of the Hacienda Bakery. The wrecker was loading her red economy car onto a flatbed tow truck. Marco parked across the dingy street. "You two can stay—"

Paloma hopped out of the back seat and waved her arm in a sweeping arc. "Hey, Mom, we're here!" Spring smiled as she crossed the street with Paloma.

What is this—a party? Marco brought up the rear. He approached the heavy, bearded man in khaki work clothes. "What was the problem?"

The man shrugged. "Her car just decided to die here. You'll have to ask the mechanic for a diagnosis." The man was holding a clipboard and handed Marco's mother the yellow copy. "I'm ready to take off. Good timing."

Marco's mother thanked the man, who then slid into the cab of the Tomaso's Towing truck and drove away with a grinding of gears and a loud rumbling of the heavy-duty engine.

"Marco, I'm so sorry I had to call you." His

mother looked at Paloma, then her eyes slid to Spring. "And why aren't you in school, Paloma?"

Marco tried to recall if he had ever mentioned his knowing "Matilde's Spring" to his mother. He didn't want her to start matchmaking again. In the past two years, a series of pretty girls had "dropped in" while he was visiting his mother. He was sure they'd been invited.

"It may take some time to sort out." Spring offered her hand. "I'm Spring Kirkland."

Marco grimaced. He couldn't focus his mind. He should have thought to introduce them.

"You're Matilde's Spring? *Ay!* I feel like I know you. Matilde has talked about you since you were a little girl." His mother glanced from him to her, as though trying to read their minds. "Did you two meet at Golden Sands? I didn't know that you knew one another."

Spring smiled. "Marco and I went to the university at the same time. We had a few classes together. I met him again at the country club recently."

"You did?" His mother eyed him.

Marco nodded, hoping his mother wouldn't jump to conclusions. Spring was out of his league, and he knew it.

"Yes, now I'm giving Marco a few golf lessons." Spring chuckled.

"You are?" His mother goggled at him.

"Mom," Paloma interrupted, "Marco's taking us to Mamacita's for lunch."

Marco was steaming inside. He wanted Spring

home and himself safely at the hospital checking on Mr. Gardner. "I didn't say that. I don't think Mother wants you rewarded for having been—"

"It's just lunch," Spring cut in with a bright smile. "We have to eat, Marco."

Why had Spring stopped him from telling his mother about Paloma's suspension?

Before Marco could make the three females realize that he would not take them to Mamacita's for a late lunch, the four of them were sitting down at a booth in the back.

"Oh, just smell all those lovely spices, cilantro, cumin, chili pepper. Mmm." Spring beamed. "Did you know my sister is a professional food writer?"

"Cool!" Paloma exclaimed. "What kind of food?"

"Everything. This is just the kind of place she loves. When she takes a road trip, she always stops at cafés like this and get recipes from the local cooks."

Marco sat stiff and uncomfortable. As the day progressed, he'd felt as though control had slipped through his fingers. Like coming to Mamacita's. He'd eaten at this little café so many times, but seeing Spring, so blond, so elegant, across from him made him feel… He couldn't explain it. It just didn't feel right.

"Hey, Marco," Lupe, Mamacita's daughter, greeted him, "long time no see."

He nodded to her.

"You finally bring a woman with you—but did you

have to bring along your mother and sister as *dueñas*.'' Lupe, a cute-enough brunette in tight jeans, chuckled at her own joke.

Paloma spoke up. ''This is Spring Kirkland. Isn't that a great name?''

''Sure is. Hello, Spring, I'm Lupe. What do you want for lunch?''

''What should I order, Marco?'' Spring looked to him.

Ignoring the disconcerting effect of her clear blue eyes on him, he shrugged. ''Everything's good.''

Lupe put one hand on her hip. ''Don't sound so enthusiastic, silly man, *tonto*. Why don't you have the combo platter, Spring, since you haven't been here before.''

''Fine.'' Spring handed Lupe her menu. ''I'm unusually hungry today.''

''The combo will take care of that!'' Lupe quickly wrote down the other three orders and left to get their beverages.

''Now I want to know why Paloma is not in school.'' Mother looked across at her daughter sternly.

Paloma's face fell.

Marco opened his mouth to explain, but halted.

Shaking her head at him, Spring touched Paloma's shoulder. When his sister looked up, Spring nodded, encouraging her.

''Mom, I was suspended from school.''

Mother gasped. ''What will your father say?''

Paloma looked down at the tabletop.

"He'll say," a man's voice boomed from the doorway behind them, "why are you celebrating at Mamacita's!"

Marco closed his eyes. His stepfather. *The whole family, just what I needed.* Fitting Spring into his life wouldn't work. They were from two different worlds. Today proved that.

Nothing had gone as planned. In his mind, the hospital across town beckoned him like a haven. There he was in charge and completely safe from being tempted by a woman like Spring.

"How did you know we were here?" Mother asked.

"When I didn't find you where you said you were, I stopped at the halfway house. Someone saw you walking here." Santos grabbed a chair from an adjacent table and swung it to the booth. Focused on Paloma, he sat down, looking grim. "Now, daughter, what did you get in trouble for?"

Spring said, "Perhaps you'd like me to leave while you discuss this?"

Santos did a double take, then stood up hastily. "*Pardone.* I didn't see you there, miss."

"I'm—"

Paloma interrupted her. "This is Spring Kirkland, Matilde's Spring."

His face brightened. "Matilde is an old friend. It is an honor to meet you, *señorita*. Matilde has watched you grow up." He shook the hand Spring offered him.

"Spring came to school with Marco and picked me

up, Dad,'' Paloma admitted, holding her chin high. ''I'm very sorry about being suspended. I just lost my cool.''

Marco couldn't believe his ears. Where had his defiant sister gone?

''We will discuss this at home.'' Santos gave Paloma a stern look. ''Now! The job I did this morning made me wish I was two men, and I'm hungry enough to eat for both of them.''

''Good.'' Lupe laughed as she came up behind him, grinning. ''I put in an order for the *Grande* platter you always order.'' The waitress set down soft drinks for all of them and moved on to another table.

''I thought this was going to be a dreadful day,'' his mother said. ''Santos had that emergency call. My car broke down. And Paloma had to be picked up from school. But somehow everything looks better at Mamacita's.''

''And I got to meet all of you, too,'' Spring added with a smile.

Marco kept a straight face. He didn't share his mother's sentiments.

After a leisurely lunch, Santos went on to another job, and Marco dropped his mother and sister off at home. He'd wanted to drop Spring at her door first, but his sister needed to be home in time for an after-school baby-sitting job.

He drove, keeping his eyes on the street. In a few moments, he'd have Spring at home and he'd be on his way to the hospital. He felt he was about to round third base and reach home plate at last.

"Well." Spring sighed with satisfaction. "I think we made a good start on golf, in spite of everything." She touched his arm. "Are you really that upset about Paloma getting into a scrape at school?"

His arm tingled at her touch as he tried to think of what to say. What did she want him to say?

"What's wrong? Tell me," she prompted softly.

He glanced into her eyes cautiously. "No. I don't think my sister will do it again."

"Then, what has upset you?"

"Upset?" He frowned.

"You've been on edge all day. What's wrong? Is there something, a patient, on your mind?"

Something on his mind! Spring's nearness for most of a day had worn down his defenses. He longed to lift her hair like spun gold and feel its softness on his fingertips. "Wrong?" he managed to mumble.

"You've been preoccupied. I…I don't know how to describe it exactly. You just haven't been fully with your family, with me today." She gazed at him as though trying to will him to speak.

He struggled against his awareness of her. She smelled of gardenias like the ones his mother grew in her backyard. The scent had taunted him all day. "I just have so much to do and today was wasted—"

"The day wasn't wasted. Your sister needed you and you were there to help her. You ate a meal with your family. I don't get to do that very often anymore, usually just on holidays. Your sister will soon be in college, then married and living in another city or state—before you know it. It was a good day, Marco.''

He tried to process her words. ''Spring, I—''

His cell phone rang.

Chapter Seven

Marco nearly pitched the phone out the open car window. Groaning inside, he flipped it open by his ear. "Yes!"

"Marco, it's Lupe. I'm here with Aunty, *Tía* Rosita. She is weak and nauseated. She looks awful!"

Tía should be fine. What's changed since the last time I checked on her? "Has she been taking her medication?"

"I asked her that, and she insists she has been taking it, but I know something is wrong. Will you come?"

No, I want to take Spring home! "Yes, I'll come right over." He snapped the phone shut, then dragged his eyes once more toward the dangerously lovely lady beside him. He'd thought his "ordeal" had been about to end. "I'm sorry. It's an emergency. I have to go straight—"

"Of course. Don't mind me. I don't have to be home at any special time."

Trying to shore up his defenses against the alluring Spring, he turned left at the next green light and headed straight back to the old neighborhood where they'd eaten lunch. Lupe had a level head and wouldn't call with a false alarm.

Spring pulled her own cell phone out of her purse. Today had shaped up better than she ever could have planned. Marco had been forced to let her into his life as more than a mere acquaintance. God's hand had been busy all day!

"Hello, Matilde, it's Spring. I won't be home until late. Marco has been called to an emergency and he doesn't have time to drop me home. If he has to stay long, I can always call a cab. Okay. Bye."

"I'll get you home. Don't worry."

Spring glanced at him. Between buildings, she glimpsed the mid-winter sun slipping toward the Gulf of Mexico. Gold and violet streaked the sky. She'd spent the day with Marco and it had been wonderful! If only she could guess what he was thinking...if he was thinking about her.

"You still do house calls? I thought that was a thing of the past."

"This is a special case." He concentrated on his driving through the tourist-clogged traffic, still trying to ignore the fragrance of gardenias that wafted from her.

"How so?"

"This is an old friend of the family." *Tía* had given

him, as a ten-year-old, the job of running errands and had paid him with cookies. "*Tía* emigrated from Cuba in the sixties and retired last year at age sixty-five. For some reason, her paperwork has gotten misplaced or hung up on someone's desk in the Social Security system. She should be on medicare, but every time she applies, the computer—"

"Spits her out." Spring folded one lovely leg under her and angled herself toward him.

His self-discipline was getting a workout today! Training his eyes forward again, he nodded, a grim set to his jaw. "Yes, I think that describes it. I've written letters, made calls, submitted forms—"

"But every effort to get her benefits activated fails." She laid her slender arm along the top of the seat, her hand only inches from his shoulder.

"That sums it up." His words were curt.

Why? Was it the heavy traffic? Or was he irritated because he hadn't been able to drop her off and go back to the hospital? She had a feeling his whole life revolved around the hours he spent there. He'd even used a hospital benefit—a golf tournament—to justify taking time to learn golf.

Aunty, Eleanor and Verna Rae were right. Whether Marco and she "connected" romantically or not, he needed to get a life.

He clung doggedly to their conversation. "You sound like you have some experience with this type of government tangle. How?"

"I told you my father is a pastor. When he pastored a large church in Milwaukee, something like this would pop up occasionally. One time, I remember he spent one solid day in the local Social Security Office trying to get a widow with two small children her survivor benefits.'' She raked her fingers through her glorious hair.

He clenched his jaw, resolved to get this emergency call over and end this exquisite torture. He turned his thoughts back to what she'd said about her father's efforts. ''Did he succeed?''

''Not until he'd spent weeks following up on it—phone call after phone call. Fortunately, our church had some generous members who supported the woman until the benefits finally started.''

With relief, he pulled into the alley behind the Hacienda Bakery. *Tía* needed him and he needed to get a time-out from being alone with Spring. ''I think you should come in with me.''

''I planned to.'' Spring got out of the car and followed him toward the back staircase.

The unappetizing smells in the alley from the Dumpster made him hurry up the outside wooden staircase behind Spring.

''I've eaten up your day with my family—and now this.''

She grinned at him. ''You forgot to complain about the time I wasted on your golf lesson.''

He shook his head at her. It wasn't only him. Spring hadn't acted like herself all day.

On the top step, Lupe waited. ''I apologize if I spoiled your plans. I didn't want to call you. In fact, *Tía* is really upset with me about it. But I came over to check on her before going home for the day, and she just looked *so bad*."

Spring smiled at Lupe. "No problem. We didn't have any definite plans." *That's for sure.*

Focusing on his purpose, Marco ushered them ahead of him into the flat above the bakery where *Tía* had worked for more than thirty-five years. The uncomfortably warm apartment was small and crowded with furniture. *Tía* never parted with anything. How would Spring handle this?

Marco heard *Tía* comforting her cat, Alejandro, and called out, "*Tía*, how do you feel?"

"*Terrible.*"

He grinned to himself. At least *Tía* hadn't lost her spicy tongue. A good sign. Walking into the tiny kitchen, he dropped his small medical bag on the kitchen table. *Tía* sat on a straight chair in a faded pink housedress. Round and full-cheeked, she *looked* like a woman who'd worked in a bakery most of her life.

He touched *Tía*'s forehead. *Warm, flushed and dry—not good.* He pinched the skin on her forehead.

"Don't do that," she scolded.

His pinch of her skin remained "tented" for several seconds before it sank back to normal. *Loss of skin elasticity.* He felt as if he were reading the textbook symptoms of uncontrolled diabetes. But Lupe had said *Tía* insisted she'd been taking her oral medications.

He dug into his bag, then put the blood-pressure cuff around her arm.

"You fuss so much, Marco. I'm just a little run down…"

He frowned as her voice trailed off. Her eyes wandered as if she couldn't focus. *Changes in the level of consciousness,* his mind went on, reciting the list of symptoms. He eyed the blood-pressure gauge: 105/70. *Bad.* He frowned. "*Tía,* have you been taking your pills regularly and testing yourself?"

"Of course, Marco. Who came with you?" The old woman looked past him to where Lupe and Spring stood side by side.

Had *Tía* just noticed Spring? That was a danger signal in itself. *Tía* never missed anything.

Marco unwrapped a sterile lancet and pricked *Tía*'s middle finger to do a blood-glucose test. *Glucose running way too high. What had brought this on?* "Lupe, please get me her bottle of pills from the refrigerator."

Lupe handed him the amber plastic bottle of pills.

He studied the date and number of pills listed on the pharmacy label. Today was in the last week of February. The bottle should be almost empty. It was half full. He fumed. Didn't she understand how serious her diabetes was? He held the bottle in front of her face.

"You haven't been taking your pills."

"I have—"

Spring leaned closer. "Perhaps you've only been taking them every other day?"

After gazing at Spring for a moment, *Tía* nodded, looking ready to burst into tears.

Marco's patience cracked. "But you have to take them every day!"

Tía's face twisted with distress. "How can I, Marco? I need heart pills. I need diabetes pills. I have arthritis. I'm good for nothing, and medicare says *Tía* doesn't live here." The old woman jabbed her thumb at herself. "But here I am! So much for government officials. Some of them remind me of ones I left behind in Cuba forty years ago!"

Marco dropped his blood-pressure and blood-glucose kits back into his bag and snapped it shut. "*Tía*, I need to take you to the hospital."

"No, no." Her voice rose shrilly. "I can't pay—"

"If I wait any longer, we'll need to call an ambulance and that will cost even more money!" Marco declared in no uncertain terms.

"Maybe I just wait for the hearse to come for me." *Tía* folded her plump arms over her bulky middle. "Then I won't have to worry about how hard I worked for over thirty years, and now medicare—"

"*Tía*," Lupe began, "don't say—"

Spring stepped to *Tía*'s side and took her hand. "Please come now. You don't want to make the EMTs carry you out. Just think of those steep stairs. I wouldn't want to be carried on a stretcher down them. Do you?"

Tía studied Spring. She sighed. "No, I wouldn't like that."

Spring gently coaxed *Tía* onto her feet.

Tía glanced around. "Have you seen my cat?"

"No, do you want me to look for her?"

"He's a he-cat, Alejandro." *Tía* called the name, but no cat appeared.

"While Marco and I help you down the steps, perhaps Lupe could find Alejandro, turn off your lights and lock up."

"Sure," Lupe agreed.

Tía reached for an oversize black purse on the countertop. "That would be good. Lupe needs to get home and cook for her family."

"Then, we shouldn't keep her," Spring said.

Amazed, Marco listened as Spring charmed the stubborn old woman into agreeing with his orders. He'd never guessed at this side of Spring.

"Should we feed Alejandro?" Spring held *Tía*'s hand in both of hers, as the old woman lumbered through her apartment.

"No, I fed him just before Lupe came." Still, she scanned the room as though looking for something.

"And he has enough water for the evening?" Spring reached over and took down a sweater from a hook beside the door.

The old woman grunted. "*Gracias,* I was looking for that."

Lupe said, "Don't worry. I'll take care of everything."

"*Gracias,* Lupita." As the old woman leaned on Spring, she tottered the last few paces to the door.

Draping the sweater around *Tía*'s wide shoulders, Spring sent Marco a glance, and he hurried forward to open the door for them.

In a gentle voice, Marco cautioned, "Now, we

don't have to rush down these steps. You set the pace and I'll follow it. Spring, would you please go down beside *Tía?* Then *Tía* can put one hand on my back, while you support her on one side.''

They obeyed him. The three of them connected by their hands made a slow, halting, procession, step by step, down the rickety stairs. The wood creaked with the combined weight of Spring and *Tía* on the same step. Finally at the bottom, Marco unlocked the back seat door, and Spring helped *Tía* sit and swing her legs inside.

Tía heaved a loud sigh. "Marco, you've found yourself a sweet girl.'' Looking drained, she leaned her bulk back against the seat.

The old woman's words hit a nerve. But now wasn't the time to tell her that her assumption that Spring and he were a couple was wrong. Better for now to just to let her think what she wished.

His patient's deteriorating condition needed all his attention. He didn't like the lack of sweat on her brow.

"I'll sit in the back with her,'' Spring murmured. She followed him to the other side of the car and climbed in.

This accomplished, Marco drove down the length of the alley and onto busy Main Street. As he drove, he observed in the rearview mirror that Spring was taking *Tía*'s hand. He had never doubted that Spring was a good person, but he'd never imagined she could fit in with people so unlike her. It was a revelation to him.

She held *Tía*'s hand all the way to the hospital. He pulled up at the emergency doors and parked. Spring hopped out of the car without his assistance and met him at *Tía*'s door. With his arms under hers, he helped the old woman out of the back seat and into a wheelchair outside the door.

"Do you want me to help her inside while you park the car, or should I park the car?" Spring asked.

"My reserved space is just around the corner. I'll park and meet you inside." He walked briskly to the car and drove off.

By the time he entered the emergency doors, Spring had already piloted *Tía* to the counter and was speaking to two nurses. One held a clipboard and pen. The other gripped *Tía*'s wrist as she took a pulse.

He hurried to them. "Let's get this patient on an IV drip of 0.45 normal saline. Get me a current weight, and I'll have the insulin order for you in a second—"

The nurse with the clipboard said, "Of course, we'll treat her immediately. But she says she has no insurance or medicare. You know we have to put down some guarantor—"

Spring leaned close to the nurse and whispered just loud enough for the nurse and him to hear, "I'm sure my aunt, Geneva Dorfman, will take care of this."

"Oh." The nurse's eyes widened. "Of course, then."

The other nurse said, "Her pulse is weak and thready." She took the wheelchair over from Spring. "*Señora,* I need to weigh you, then start that IV."

"She looks like she's lost weight to me," Marco observed.

"I don't want to get weighed. I know I'm too heavy," *Tía* grumbled, as the nurse pushed her away in the wheelchair.

Spring turned to him. "Is there anything else I can do?"

He held her upper arms. She'd helped this emergency call go so smoothly. He didn't know how to thank her.

She put one hand on his and nodded. Her tender expression twisted something inside him, and a rush of emotion flowed through him. Suddenly, he wanted to kiss her. He turned abruptly away and went to his patient.

Over the next few minutes, Marco concentrated on treating and stabilizing *Tía* Rosita. Finally, he helped heft her onto a gurney, which would take her up to a room. He walked beside it toward the elevator.

"But, Marco, I don't have any money for this!" *Tía* complained once more.

"Don't worry." Spring trailed along on her other side. "We'll sort this all out in the morning."

The old woman's face crinkled up, ready to cry. "But—"

"*Tía*, you don't have a choice." He started to give her a good scare. "Neither of us wants the alternative. Let's just get you on your feet—"

Spring interrupted him. "Don't you think God is capable of providing for you?" She grasped *Tía*'s hand again. "You must trust in God about this. He loves you and He will see that you are taken care of.''

The panic drained away from *Tía*'s expression. ''I'm a forgetful old woman.'' She shook her head. ''God has brought me through much.''

Spring squeezed the gnarled hand. ''Then, don't doubt Him now.'' She quoted, '' 'God is able to provide exceedingly beyond what we ask for.' Don't forget that. Now just rest and do what the nurses tell you to. I'll come and visit you in the morning, and tonight I will include you in my prayers.''

Tía's face puckered with tears of gratitude. ''God bless you, *señorita.*''

Marco echoed this silently.

The orderly wheeled the gurney onto the elevator. Stepping inside, Marco took the last bit of room. ''Spring, do you mind waiting here? I'll be right down to take you home.''

''Of course. *Buenas noches, Tía.*'' Giving a warm smile, she waved.

About ten minutes later, after clarifying his instructions, Marco found Spring chatting to two nurses near the emergency doors. The nurses looked up at him with peculiar expressions and funny little smiles. What did that mean? Did they think it odd that someone like Spring would be hanging around with him?

Looking unconcerned, Spring rose and wished them goodbye. With a polite nod to them, he escorted her to his car. ''I'll take you home now.'' Taking her home had been his goal since late morning. Now he could do it, but why was his mood sliding to somber?

She glanced at her watch. "We missed dinner. Why don't we stop at the Greek restaurant again?"

Marco heaved a long breath. He had to get her home before he did something that would betray his interest in her. She'd been so caring, so wonderful today, his feelings for her had grown way beyond what was appropriate. "Don't take this the wrong way, but I'm just too stressed to sit in a restaurant."

His reply daunted Spring. She'd felt them drawing nearer to each other, and his words made her feel as if she'd been pushed away. Forcing herself not to slip back inside her shell, Spring considered how Doree or even Hannah would handle this. She stiffened her resolve and suggested, "Why don't we go to your place and order in?"

Entering Marco's town house, Spring looked around at the stark interior. *It's nearly empty!*

He must have read her mind because he explained, "I haven't had the time…or the inclination to decorate."

Her mother always said single men only "camp out" in a place. It took a woman to make a home. Spring said with a positive lilt, "You have a good amount of space to work with."

Scanning the layout of the first floor with its narrow entry hall, great room and small eat-in kitchen, she tried to imagine it with furniture. She walked to a lawn chair that sat facing out the sliding glass doors to the darkened backyard. "I should come over and place some pots of flowers around the patio for you.

At least you'd have something cheerful to look at when you got home at night.''

Marco didn't know how to reply. He'd never brought anyone to his apartment. How had she gotten him to bring her here? The answer came to him, but wasn't what he wanted to hear. After spending all day and into the evening with her, he'd been loath to take her home. Spring's cheerful presence exerted a power over him that had grown and strengthened, just as he had feared. Her sensitivity had been so helpful, so unanticipated. She even made his forlorn town house look better, just standing in it. He no longer wanted to take her home.

"*Tía* will be all right, won't she?"

Grateful for this safe subject, he nodded. "She should be. She'll have to be in the hospital a few days, so I can get her blood-sugar levels stabilized. How did you guess she had been taking only one pill every other day."

Spring sighed. "It's the kind of thing people of her generation do. They don't understand how not taking medicine correctly will affect their medical condition, and they think they will save money. But in *Tía*'s situation, she had an understandable motive—her frustration over her medicare glitch."

She moved closer to the sliding glass doors, gazing out at the pools of light illuminating the path between the town houses. He couldn't take his eyes from her.

She glanced back at him and smiled. "But my father had to deal with older parishioners, some who had plenty of money and medicare, and they still couldn't bring themselves to spend the co-payment for their medication. Father explained to me that it wasn't just surviving the Depression.''

"What is it, then?'' he asked.

"The seniors of today were raised at a time when doctors had few effective drugs available. I mean, sixty years ago penicillin was just in its infancy. In our grandparents' youth, medicine was more of an art than a science. It's our generation that expects medical miracles and sues if we don't get them!''

"I'd never thought of it that way.'' And it was true. Her explanation made some frustrating conversations he'd had with older patients comprehensible.

She grinned at him. "I'm hungry. What should we order?''

Shouldn't he suggest they go to a decent restaurant, after all? It was so hard to figure out how to handle this newly discovered Spring. "What do you want?''

"I've been longing for pizza!'' She spun around and faced him. "My aunt's only failing is that she doesn't like pizza. Again, ordering pizza wasn't an option when Aunty was growing up.''

"Pizza, it is, then. How about Antonio's on Canal Street?'' He opened the *Yellow Pages*. "What do you like on your pizza?'' This seemed a surreal conversation. Ordering pizza with Spring Kirkland in his unfurnished town house. What did she think of that?

"What do you prefer?''

"The works,'' he said firmly.

"Just the way I like it, too. '' She lowered herself gracefully into one of the lawn chairs.

Sitting down on a nearby lawn chair, he handed her the phone and let her give the order. He felt himself grinning but couldn't stop himself.

When she was done, she smiled back at him.

He swallowed a huge, dry lump in his throat.

Spring ran her fingers lightly through her hair. "We've had quite a busy day."

To say the least! He wondered if her hair would feel as soft as he imagined. "I'm sorry to take up your—"

"I didn't mind. I needed a day away from Matilde and Aunty. I love them both, but having two mother hens clucking around me all day for several weeks…" She gave an exaggerated shrug.

"Well, you'll be going home soon, won't you?" The words clouded his mood and rang an alarm inside him. *Spring is only here on a visit. Get used to it.*

"I don't know." She frowned. "I know you're not supposed to give out information about patients." She glanced at him. "But I'm concerned for my aunt. How serious is her condition?"

Rising, he turned his gaze to the night, which had closed in around them. "You're right. I can't tell you that unless she's given you medical power of attorney."

She nodded. "I won't press you, then."

"Why did you say your aunt would take care of *Tía*'s medical care?"

She looked surprised, as though he shouldn't have to ask this. "She's done that on and off over the years, both here and up north. Often, my father or mother would call her and she would send a check to our church benevolence fund, which would then pay for needed medical attention for some person without insurance.''

''I never knew.'' Though he should have guessed. After all, the generosity of the members of Golden Sands had benefited him. It was a debt of honor he'd never be able to repay.

''Oh, Aunt Geneva has a big heart. You know she paid for all my operations.''

''Operations?'' This startled him, and he turned to her.

''Yes, I was born with a clubfoot.'' She motioned toward her trim ankles. ''Aunty paid for all the operations so I could walk. I forget how many surgeries I had before I was five. But it took many years before I was able to walk into a hospital without experiencing real panic.''

He tried to process this. He'd never thought of Spring as a person born with a serious handicap. It didn't fit her. ''Your parents didn't have health insurance?''

''Of course, they had some, but my operations were so costly we had to have help. I told you that you didn't really understand my family. The fact Aunt Geneva is wealthy has nothing to do with the rest of us.''

He took a step closer as he tried to adjust his thinking.

She moved toward him. ''Then, just when I got done with all my operations, I came down with asthma. Since I have the type of asthma that is worse in cold weather, I spent several winters here with Aunt Geneva and Uncle Howie. Fortunately, I outgrew it, but that's why Aunt Geneva and I are so close. She has been a second grandmother to me. And, of course, Matilde is like an aunt to me."

Her nearness worked on him like mesmerism. "So your family isn't wealthy?"

She chuckled. "You're a slow learner, Doctor. Now do you understand the kind of family I came from? It probably isn't very much different from your family."

This he did not believe, but he didn't say so. The fragrance of gardenias drew him to her. She glowed like burnished copper in the low light. He couldn't stop himself. He took another step closer to her.

"Isn't there a free clinic here?"

Spring's out-of-the-blue question rendered him speechless.

"Is something wrong?" She leaned nearer.

"Why would you ask that?" He had trouble getting the words out.

"Because after what happened with *Tía* Rosita tonight, I think there should be one. Would you talk to some other doctors about starting one? Often if several health-care professionals band together in an area, they can get one off the ground. It has a positive effect on a community."

Her question had sliced his chest open and bared his heart. He could barely speak. "That's been my dream."

She stood right next to him. He stared at her rich golden-brown lashes. She was close enough to kiss. He tilted his head.

She gazed at him. "Really?"

The pizza delivery boy chose that moment to knock on the door. Marco turned, putting aside the chaos Spring's nearness and her innocent question had unleashed. A few minutes passed while the transaction—money exchanged for pizza and soft drinks—took place.

"Mmm. This smells delicious. I've been so hungry today! Usually I have very little appetite." Spring surprised him by carrying the pizza out onto the patio. "Bring out the chairs. Let's eat *al fresco.*"

Still bemused by her presence, he carried out the chairs, and they sat down in the dim light and popped open their soda cans. Spring lifted a huge slice of pizza loaded with everything on it, smiled at him, then took her first bite.

Entranced, he followed suit. The pizza woke his empty stomach with a jolt—just as Spring had charmed his stressful day. *Spring, you are more wonderful than I knew or ever guessed.* He couldn't say anything at first. He could only chew and gaze at the beautiful and sensitive woman in the shadows beside him.

She lowered her slice of pizza. "So tell me about your dream."

Chapter Eight

With the first tangy bite of pizza on his tongue, Marco froze. How could he answer her? He'd only shared this with his mother...and God.

"You don't have to tell me. I didn't mean to pry."

Her sensitive apology pulled the linchpin that had held back his voice. "When I got the chance to buy Dr. Johnson's practice, I realized that I would be in a position to be of service to my community sooner than if I'd had to slowly build my own practice."

She nodded. Marco let the balmy evening wrap itself around them. It was easy to imagine them far away from others on a twilight island. A very pleasant sensation. Her flaxen hair caught the lamplight and glowed like a halo. A dribble of tomato sauce decorated the corner of her mouth.

The sight made her more endearing than he'd thought possible. He couldn't help himself. He reached over and dabbed it away with his napkin.

Grinning, she submitted. "Thanks. Go on. Please."

"Well, *Tía* Rosita is only one of many people who need short-term medical care—"

"People who slip between the cracks?"

Her encouragement urged him on. "Yes, people who've lost their jobs, people who've just immigrated, people whose paperwork gets lost by medicaid or medicare—"

"Exactly." She finished her slice. "What have you done so far?"

Sated by the tasty pizza, he wiped his face and hands.

Her matter-of-fact attitude made it much easier to bring this subject so close to his heart out into the open. "I've been looking around for a site."

"In the old downtown?"

He glanced at her. "Right." How had she guessed that?

Nodding, she supplied the answer to his unspoken question. "Real estate's cheaper and the location's accessible to more prospective patients and public transportation."

Her incisive comments once more caught him by surprise. "That's true."

"Did you find a place?"

Her unexpected interest in his dream and her nearness made him vibrate inside like a plucked guitar string. He leaned forward in the low light, wanting to see the excitement on her face more clearly. "Yes, there's a vacant church on Van Buren."

She shook her head and rested her back against the

chair. "I always hate to see a congregation move out of its building."

In the duskiness, her white shorts and her long pale legs reflected the scant light. She took on an ethereal quality, like a fairy princess. The effect made his mouth dry.

"They outgrew their facility."

"Then, they should have planted another church in another neighborhood and helped it get off the ground. Then this community would have two churches instead of one and one empty building." She shook her head in disapproval. "But parishioners move out of the original neighborhood. The neighborhood itself changes...."

The common excuse for moving away from people deemed "undesirable" hit him smack between the eyes. Jolted back to reality, he gave a harsh laugh. "Changes. You mean the residents become undesirable."

"Unfortunately, that's often the case." Spring sat up and leaned forward, too, her elbows resting on the plastic chair arms. "But it's often hard for people to look past surface differences—and if there's a language barrier, the gulf can be hard to bridge. And when property values drop, it brings crime."

He brushed these excuses aside. "Let's face it. There are just different kinds of people. New immigrants have always been shunned in America." He couldn't keep the bitterness from his voice.

Looking wounded, Spring bowed her head as though praying. She looked up. "Some of what you say is true. But I think you're judging people by your preconceptions rather than by reality. You shouldn't give in to prejudice.''

He gasped. He couldn't believe his ears. ''Prejudice! Me?''

She nodded. ''Perhaps you've been wounded in the past by some people who lack understanding and love for others.''

''Sheesh. You *are* a pastor's daughter.'' How could she ignore all the people who looked down on anyone with darker skin or an accent?

She frowned. ''What do you mean?''

Marco scowled. ''I mean…'' What did he mean? Could he tell her he thought her idealistic, completely unrealistic? How could he?

After a few weighty moments of heavy silence passed, Spring looked into his eyes. Laughter from a distant patio contrasted with her serious expression. ''So how are you going to pay for the church?''

He broke eye contact. ''I don't know. I've been trying to figure out how to come up with the down payment.''

''Yourself?'' She made it sound as if he'd said something ridiculous. ''That doesn't make sense.''

Almost offended by her sharp tone, he raised his eyebrows at her. ''What do you mean?''

''You can't do a project like this all by yourself. Even if you could raise a down payment by yourself, how would you come up with the monthly payments or pay for improvements?''

She'd brought up the questions he'd most wanted

to avoid. "I wasn't planning on doing it all by myself. I thought I might interest another doctor or two. I've been praying about that."

She leaned closer with a coaxing smile. "Then, it's time to step out and expect God to do wonders. Definitely, a few more doctors would help, but you need other—"

Marco shook his head. "I don't want to be one of those people who goes around with his hand out—"

She grimaced. "Then, you might as well put the idea away for many, many years. You may finally make enough money to do this all alone or with another doctor. But it could take twenty years or more."

"What do you suggest?"

Stretching her arms overhead as though tired, she smiled at him. "So glad you asked. You don't realize that you're talking to a professional fund-raiser."

She wasn't making sense. "You work at the Botanical Gardens!"

Lowering her arms, she pointed to herself. "I'm the community relations director. My job is to bring the public to the gardens, and that often includes raising money for different exhibits. I'm just the lady you were looking for."

"I don't see—"

She held up both hands, halting him. "That's because you don't have a plan."

"A plan?"

"Before you can go about raising money, you must have a plan." She began ticking off on her fingers, one by one. "A plan that shows your goals, the good you intend to do, how much is needed and your methods to achieve the clinic.''

He stared at her, speechless. How could he put this special, secret dream onto a chart for everyone to see?

She smiled back at him. ''After you draw up your plan, you need to get in touch with prospective donors. It's quite easy, you see.''

He didn't see. He regretted exposing his deep aspirations to her. How could he just open up to strangers the way she expected?

''Oh! I just had a wonderful idea. I know where we can start looking for contributors.'' Before he could stop her, she jumped up and hurried back inside. Returning within minutes, she was talking into her cell phone. ''That's wonderful, Mimi. I can't wait. Great!'' She hung up and clapped her hands. ''We're in luck.''

''Luck?''

''Yes, our university's annual spring alumni cruise has had a last-minute cancellation. There's a cabin open for you!''

Late, after his office hours the next afternoon, Marco walked into his mother's fragrant kitchen. *''Buenas tardes, Mama.''*

She stood by the stove stirring a pot, the contents of which filled the air with the fragrance of chili pepper. ''Marco, *hola.* What brings you by?''

He leaned against the worn countertop and tried to think of an answer. Spring Kirkland and her outrageous proposal popped up immediately. He couldn't believe he'd uncovered his dream to her. And now a cruise—she wanted him to reveal himself to people who'd shunned him in college. Never! Shaking his head, he glanced into the dinette.

"How's Paloma?"

"She's in her room studying until Santos comes home."

"Is that her penalty for being suspended?" Marco had been concerned about this, hoping Santos wouldn't precipitate another crisis with a harsher punishment.

"She's grounded for another week—except for her Saturday job." She spooned up a bit of bean mixture, then blew on it to cool it before tasting.

The mention of the job tightened his nerves. "Why is Paloma working? If she needs help for college, I'll—"

"Son, Santos's business is doing well." She shook more salt into the pot. "We are well able to pay for her education."

"Then, why is she being sent out to work as a domestic?"

"Marco!" his mother scolded. "Work is good. What is the shame in helping Matilde by doing the heavier jobs? Matilde is nearly sixty now."

When he made no reply, she continued, "I'm sorry you had to work as hard as you did, but you chose to go into medicine. That's much more expensive than just a four-year degree. And Santos was just establishing his business. Otherwise, when you were in college, we'd have helped you more."

Marco felt his jaw clench. "My education wasn't Santos's responsibility."

His mother made a sound of irritation. "After all this time, you still haven't accepted Santos. Why? He's a good man. He cares about you."

Every word she said rang true, but he couldn't change his feelings. They'd solidified too many years ago. When he thought of his stepfather, his heart always felt laden, rock hard. "I have no argument with your husband. He's just not my father."

"He's your stepfather. Without him, I'd still be living in Spanish Town. He's always tried to make you feel a part of this family, but you always hold back. Why?"

His mother turned her heated gaze upon him, and he felt the full impact of her words. But he still couldn't put his response to his stepfather into words. Why did it matter to her? He'd never been rude or disobedient to her husband.

Marco pushed himself away from the counter. "I'll be off then."

"No!" She pointed her ladle at him. "I'm not letting you do that anymore—walk out when the conversation doesn't go the way you want it."

His lips parted in surprise, he stared at her.

"Now, you came here to talk to me about something and you're not leaving until I hear what it is. And you're staying for dinner. No argument."

He lifted his eyes to the ceiling. First Spring. Now his mother. Thoroughly disgruntled with the women in his life, he considered leaving, anyway.

"I'm making rice, too," his mother coaxed.

Black beans and rice, his favorite. He grinned even though he didn't want to. Glancing at his mother, he took a deep breath. "Spring wants me to go on the alumni cruise with her next weekend."

His mother's mouth dropped open. "Marco!"

"You've given me my answer." He folded his arms. "It's ridiculous." He should feel relieved, but his mood only darkened more.

"A cruise. How wonderful!" His mother clasped both hands around the ladle handle. "At last, you're going to take time for yourself. And Spring—such a lovely girl and so sweet! She's wonderful!"

"This isn't what you think!" he cautioned, even as Spring's face came up vividly in his mind. "I was afraid you'd jump to the wrong conclusion." His frustration mounted. "I'm just not in her league—"

"Nonsense! You're a successful doctor with a fine practice, and I could see how her eyes lingered on you. She likes you. With just a little encouragement—"

His mother's reaction made him more than a little desperate. His heartbeat became magnified throughout his body. He couldn't let anyone know that he wanted Spring even though he was doomed to never attain her. "No! Mother, I don't have time for romance, and Spring Kirkland isn't interested in me, never will be."

His mother pursed her lips and frowned at him. "Then, why did she invite you to go on the cruise with her?"

"It's not like that. This is business." *Just business.*

"What business?" She perched both hands on her hips.

"You know the church on Van Buren I've been looking at as a possible site for my clinic?"

"*Sí.*" She turned back to the pot and stirred it.

"Spring says that I need a plan for the free clinic and I need backers. She says I can get backers on the cruise. You know, from fellow alumni."

His mother looked impressed. "That girl has a head on her shoulders. She's not just a lovely face." She nodded decisively.

He'd tried not to think of Spring just in terms of her physical beauty. *She's so much more.*

"So when do you leave?" Mother smiled at him.

"What?"

"When's the cruise?"

"I haven't agreed to go." Marco backpedaled. "It would be a huge waste of time. And an alumni cruise…it's not my kind of thing."

"Why not? Alumni means people who graduated from the same school, doesn't it? So that means you'd belong. I think a cruise would be a good thing for you to try."

I never belonged. He tried again. "But I never went in for social stuff like that at school. Spring was in a sorority." He remembered grimly the faces, the names of a few guys she'd dated. None of them had been worthy of her. "She'll want to be with her friends. I'd just be in the way."

His mother turned to face him again. "Sometimes I could just shake you." The dripping ladle waved in front of his nose. "When are you going to realize you need to get away from that hospital!"

The sound of his stepfather's car pulling into the carport made them both turn to the outside window.

"I'll be going—"

"No, you won't!" Mother grabbed his arm and waggled her ladle at him again. "You're staying for dinner and you're going to carry on a conversation with your stepfather...or...or else!"

After enjoying black beans and rice and helping Paloma with her algebra, Marco went to the hospital. He strode up the comforting, familiar hallway; all the clinical scents and sounds soothed his ruffled nerves. He wanted to check on *Tía* Rosita before going home for the night. Her glucose level still concerned him. He needed to be sure she would be able to go home tomorrow as he'd promised.

Laughter came from *Tía*'s room. *Spring's laughter*. He froze just inside the door, shock waves radiating through him.

"Marco!" *Tía* exclaimed. "Your lady friend came to see how I am!"

Lovely in a stylish blue dress, Spring turned to him. Her gaze measured him.

His pulse throbbed in his ears. He could almost hear her asking, what had he decided? He'd have to say no and make it stick. What was dearest to him couldn't be put on display before people who wouldn't understand.

Walking directly to his patient, he pasted a smile

on his face. He lifted *Tía* Rosita's chart and read the latest notes made by the nurse on duty. *Tía*'s blood-sugar numbers had stabilized. His smile became genuine.

"Everything looks excellent. You'll be home tomorrow."

"*Gracias,* Jesus." The old woman pressed her hands together.

Spring beamed. "Praise the Lord."

Tía patted Spring's hand. "This sweet girl has been telling me that you're going to go on a cruise—"

"I just said we might go on the cruise," Spring interrupted.

Marco cleared his throat, his stomach a simmering pot. He would put a stop to this right now. "I'm not going to be able to get away—"

"You must go!" *Tía* insisted. "You take no time for fun."

Marco had had enough. Didn't anybody understand? He hadn't chosen a "fun" career. People's lives depended on him. He couldn't just run off to have a good time!

Spring touched his arm, sensitizing him to her even more. "Marco, don't take *Tía* Rosita in the wrong way. You take good care of your patients. You help your sister." She smiled at him. It melted his aggravation. Did she know her power over him? "*Tía* just wants you to have a good time."

"That's right," the plump silver-haired grandmother agreed. "Now, Marco, you walk this pretty *señorita* to her car. I told her she shouldn't be out alone after dark. It's not safe.''

The ploy smacked of matchmaking, but what could he say? He bid his patient good-night. As Spring strolled at his side to the elevator, he became aware of two things. First, every nurse turned to watch them; second, he had to fight the urge to take her hand.

Spring entered the elevator first. He followed, then faced their ''audience.'' At his frown, all the nurses suddenly looked busy.

When the elevator doors closed, Spring looked down at herself. ''Do I have a button open or a stain I didn't notice?''

He ground his teeth. ''No, they just have never seen me with a woman before.''

Obviously disconcerted, Spring stared at him while the elevator dropped level by level. ''I'm sorry. I didn't come to embarrass you. I didn't know you were coming up this evening. I just wanted to visit—''

''It's all right. It's not your fault.'' He stifled his anger. If anyone was guiltless in this cosmic matchmaking, Spring was. She wasn't the kind of woman who pursued men.

The double doors opened. Spring stepped out. Walking beside her, breathing in her light floral perfume, he followed her to the exit. Their progress again elicited staff attention, not even faintly discreet.

Moments later, once more, they stood together beside her car in the dark, summer-like February evening.

Spring looked up at him. How she longed to rest

her cheek against him and feel his arms close around her. But first she had to make that possible. Even as she fought her own reticence, she had to chip away his defenses, too. Now she had to shake him out of his rut and into her life, or at least try.

"Have you made your decision?"

"I don't—"

"Please." She halted him by grasping his forearm. Her stomach did a somersault at her own forwardness, but she continued, "I'm not asking you to marry me. I just want you to go on a cruise to see if we can manage to raise funds for a free clinic I know you want. Why are you hesitating? Is it me?"

Chapter Nine

The balmy night closed softly around them as it had on his patio. Spring's heart lodged in her throat while she awaited his reply. Pressing him about the cruise... Had she pushed him too hard? Would he withdraw completely, destroying her new, tenuous link to his life? Spending the day with his family, then the evening on his patio, had drawn her rampant emotions so much closer to the surface. She'd suppressed her feelings for this proud man for so long. She was playing with fire. She could win him or lose any chance with him at all. In spite of the warm breeze, she shivered with uncertainty.

"My hesitance has nothing to do with you."

His tone begrudged her every syllable.

Praying that her voice wouldn't shake, she went on. "I'm just trying to help. A free clinic would do so much for the downtown, help so many people."

He bowed his head as though praying or searching

for words. A dove in the live oak near the entrance cooed, unseen.

She waited, silently beseeching heaven. *God, please let him break out of his reserve. Help him see what needs to be done. Let me encourage him, not just because I want to work beside him, not just because I love him, but because together we might do Your work. You are the Great Healer. Please....*

"I think your offer of help is sincere and I do accept that I need backers if this project is going to get off the ground, but..." Again he measured out each word as if it were fine gold dust.

She went on praying. One car then another drove past, looking for parking places. A blaring siren shook the quiet as an ambulance careened up to the emergency doors.

Glancing toward the hospital, he sucked in breath. "I have never gone in for social occasions. You know that—"

"I didn't, either, until Aunt Geneva insisted I pledge a sorority." Did he still see her as so different from him? She wished she could take his broad shoulders into her hands and shake him out of all his preconceptions. The thought of holding Marco worked its way through her like the warm Gulf breeze that fluttered the short tendrils around her face. She pushed them back.

"Your aunt insisted? You mean, you didn't want to?"

She shook her head. In the face of all the complexity of human beings, he'd neatly labeled everyone and put them in the slots he'd created. Didn't he see how ridiculous that was? "No, I was petrified during Rush Week. I didn't want to join something that felt out of character for me, but I didn't want to disappoint Aunty, either. Anyway, I thought no sorority would want me. I was shocked when the Deltas pledged me."

He firmed his jaw as he gazed at her.

His classic profile, cast in shadows from the street lamps high above them, filled her with longing. Why couldn't this be simpler? Why couldn't she just say, "I think I love you"? *Someday I will.*

She swallowed to moisten her dry mouth. "A few of the girls were stuck on themselves. Every group has some of those. But after attending several of the functions, I realized that some were in the same situation I was. Their mothers or grandmothers had been Deltas, and they had been pushed to pledge, too. As soon as I found that out, I relaxed and started making friends."

He nodded.

She wished she could tell what he was thinking, but his handsome face resembled a portrait of a bold and determined *conquistador,* a man accustomed to conquering city after city. She hadn't chosen the easiest man to fall in love with. Taking a deep breath, she ventured into another sensitive point. "I've been thinking that you haven't attended any alumni activities, have you?"

He shook his head.

She pursed her lips. "You haven't seen how people

change. You shouldn't think of the other alumni as college students anymore. Just as you have changed, matured, so have the people you don't think you'll fit in with. Things that might have mattered then, don't now. We're all nearly a decade older than we were in college.''

''I hadn't thought of that.'' His reply sounded more natural.

Her inner pressure eased a bit more. ''I think you'll be surprised at what a mellow group some of us have become. I still keep in close touch with four Deltas. I know their husbands, too. Some went to school with us. Some didn't. They'll all be on the cruise, and I'm looking forward to relaxing and having fun with them.''

''Won't you regret having to do fund-raising, then?'' He stretched his lean body back against her aunt's car.

''I have become accustomed to it. And talking with friends and acquaintances will make it easier. Maybe you don't realize it, but you and I are *known* quantities. Since we're all Florida U alumni, we'll have a common connection with them or their spouses. We just have to get the ball rolling, and our project will be a topic of discussion during the tour.''

Saying her plans out loud reassured her, and she hoped it would do the same for Marco. *I'm not a silly coed, Marco!* She scolded herself. *I can't help it if you're the one who makes me feel so unsure.*

She continued, ''I don't plan on doing any hard selling, if you know what I mean. We'll just circulate and, when an opportunity presents itself, you and I will introduce the topic of a free clinic. It will sell itself.''

''Do you think so?'' He stared at her.

She blushed warm under his scrutiny. ''I wouldn't mislead you, Marco. And we need to let the alumni committee know you want that cabin they're holding for you, or it might go to someone else.''

He took a big breath. ''All right. If you think the clinic will sell itself, we have to try it.''

Bottling up her joy, she suppressed the desire to fling her arms around his neck. She merely smiled and nodded. ''You might even have a good time.''

He grimaced. *That would take a miracle, Spring.*

When Spring walked in the door, Aunt Geneva and Matilde lay in wait for her. ''*Tía* Rosita called,'' Matilde started first. ''She said you were in her hospital room when Marco came.''

With a gleam in her eyes, Aunty took up the thread. ''She said you two left together.''

Spring gave them a half frown, half smile. How did *Tía* and Matilde know each other? ''You two are like the CIA. You have your contacts everywhere!''

''Tell us!'' Matilde urged. ''Did you persuade him?''

Spring nodded. ''I have to call—''

Matilde began singing ''La Cucaracha'' and doing what must have been the rumba. Not to be outdone, Aunty joined in.

''You two!'' Spring laughed, but she was caught

in crosscurrents of elation and anxiety. Would it be as easy as she'd led Marco to believe? Would he really feel more comfortable now than he had in college? Would she be able to help him raise money for the clinic? Would she and Marco have a chance to draw even closer while away from their everyday lives?

The phone rang.

Spring picked up the one in the hall. Her mother's voice took her by surprise. "H-hello," Spring stuttered.

"Did I startle you?" Mother asked.

"Yes." A worry niggled its way into Spring's mind. "Is everything all right?" She really meant, *Are you all right?*

"Everything's fine at this end. I just wanted to ask Aunt Geneva if she was up to another guest."

"You'll have to talk to her." Spring frowned. "Is Doree wanting to come down for spring break?"

"I don't know about that, but I do know *I* need a break from snow!"

Spring smiled then. She'd dreaded Doree popping up here, badgering her in person. She'd talk to Aunt Geneva about Connie Wilson again after the cruise. Maybe this time Aunty would give them something to go on. "I know what you mean. Here, I'll hand the phone to Aunty." She did so, after murmuring to her aunt that it was Mother.

Matilde nodded and rumba-ed away toward her room off the kitchen. With a grin, Spring walked down the long hallway to her own room. She won-

dered why Mother had decided to come for a visit.
Was she feeling well or not? And would this make it
harder or easier to get Aunt Geneva to open up about
Mother's natural parents? When Spring thought about
her mother's leukemia, the familiar ache tugged at her
heart.

Marco couldn't believe what he was doing. He held
the door open for Spring and followed her into Scott's
Shop for Men. He'd never shopped anywhere but department stores at the mall. Why had he let his mother
talk him into asking Spring for help choosing clothes
for the cruise?

But he'd come home and found his mother going
through his bedroom closet, exclaiming that he had
almost nothing but suits. He'd given her a key to his
town house just in case she ever needed it, but she'd
never used it before!

After scolding him for not furnishing his town
house aside from the bedroom, she'd proceeded to tell
him that he had to go shopping before he went on the
cruise. His resistance had been futile. Then she'd
talked him into calling Spring and arranging a shopping "date" for the next day after his office hours.
What was going on? He felt as if he'd been sucked
under by a relentless undertow.

Still bemused a day later, he trailed after Spring
over the luxurious maroon carpet between the neat
racks of slacks and shirts. He noticed her slender
spine. The subtle sway to her walk made it difficult

for him to draw breath. A well-dressed silver-haired salesman greeted them.

Marco didn't appreciate the man's appreciative glance at Spring. *Behave yourself, abuelo.*

Spring informed the salesman, "We're going on a weekend cruise, and Marco needs swimming trunks, a few tank tops, matching shorts, a few sport shirts and slacks."

Disgruntled, Marco listened to Spring as though she were talking about someone else.

"What is the gentleman's size?" the salesman asked.

Spring turned to him.

Marco gave his sizes, and before he knew what was happening he was in the fitting room staring at the full-length mirror. *Why am I here? I never try on clothing in a store!* He contemplated walking out and telling Spring this, but decided doing so would only make more discussion necessary. And she wouldn't understand, anyway. *Just try them on and get this over with!*

Still wearing his white dress shirt from office hours, he pulled on the electric-blue spandex trunks Spring had picked out.

"How do those look?" she asked from her chair outside by the three-way mirror.

"Like swim trunks," he growled. *Ugly ones. I look ridiculous!*

She chuckled. "Come out."

Like a condemned man, he walked out to face her.

"Oh, I like those! Don't you?"

He shrugged. He could endure them, he supposed—if he didn't look down.

"If you don't like them, I could pick out a few more."

Anything but that! "No. These are just fine." He failed to keep the revulsion from his voice.

The salesman wandered away to help another customer. Spring stood up. Coming close to him, she murmured, "If you don't want to shop here, we can go somewhere else."

The sweet scent of gardenias floated from her, calling to him to take a step closer to her.

She gazed up into his eyes.

Her eyes. So blue. So serene. Filled with such innocent appeal. "Let's get it over with," he grumbled. "I just don't want to buy a bunch of clothes I'll never wear again."

"Don't you ever go swimming? Your town house complex has two pools."

"I've never had time—"

"Let's not go there." She waved her hand as if a mosquito had buzzed in her ear. "From now on, once a week in season, you're going to go swimming."

He only half followed her words. The way her golden hair curved around her oval face and down her back became his focus. "Why?"

"Because you don't want these trunks to go to waste." She giggled at him.

Her giggle released some tightness inside him, melted his resistance to her persuading. What was it about Spring that dissolved the willpower he'd honed over time? She made him forget what he was saying. She took him shopping. She'd talked him into going on a frivolous cruise, of all things!

Spring held her breath. She'd been afraid he was about to bolt. The teasing she'd used to overcome his stiffness had always seemed to work for Doree. She'd seen her sister charm two and three males at a time with her insouciant comments. Would it work for her?

"You're the limit, you know that?" he said at last. "I hate these trunks. Get me some in navy blue, Miss Shopper."

Spring's spirits took flight. *It worked! Good old Doree!* "Yes, Mr. Shopper," she replied with a salute.

Before long, they'd agreed on a pair of navy blue (not spandex) trunks, two pairs of chinos—one mocha and one oatmeal, two coordinating knit shirts, two pair of denim shorts and two white tank tops. But shopping for a man as handsome and well-proportioned as Marco hadn't been difficult. He could make anything look good! Spring sighed with satisfaction.

"Anything else I'll need?" Marco asked with a half smile and a sardonic twist in his voice.

Remember Doree—keep it light; keep it sassy. "Just don't forget to pack your killer smile, Doctor."

Marco just stared at her.

She smiled back at him and hoped she could carry this off. Maybe she should call Doree for advice, inspiration? Two days to castoff!

* * *

Spring walked up the slanting gangway to the cruise ship. Her heart beat like the impatient waves lapping, slapping against the ship's hull. She hated feeling so nervous. Taking a deep breath, she tried to center herself in God's peace. Her mind recited, "Be anxious for nothing, but give thanks to the Lord in all things." *I am thankful. Lord, please take this frantic feeling from me.*

She dared a glance at Marco, who walked beside her. He looked intent and serious, hardly like a man about to leave for a three-day vacation! *But I probably look just as tense!* Another deep breath in and out.

Nudging him, she whispered, "This isn't a floating dentist office. Put a smile on that face."

He gave her a fierce look in return, then visibly relaxed his expression. "How's this?" he asked in an undertone.

"Much better." Though her stomach still did the flutter-kick against her ribs, she smiled in return. Appealing to God had already begun loosening her concern. If what she was doing wasn't in God's plan for Marco, her and the clinic, she'd find out soon enough. The old hymn "Trust and Obey" played in her mind: "Never fear, only trust and obey." The tension inside her began dissolving like sugar in water.

"Spring! Spring Kirkland!" a voice hailed her from above.

Shading her eyes, Spring scanned the ship's deck. At first, she couldn't make out any faces, then she recognized the person who was waving to her. A smile lifted her face, and happiness poured through her like warm sunbeams. "Mimi! Mimi! I see you! Hi!"

Mimi, a petite redhead, waved again, leaning over the railing. "Spring, I knew you'd be early! Come on! I've already got the ball rolling. Is that Marco with you?"

Spring bobbed her head yes and stepped up her pace. "Marco, do you remember Mimi Stacey?"

"No, I don't think so."

She dragged at his arm, hurrying him along. "She was my roommate my last two years at Florida. She married Jeff Handelan. Do you remember him?"

Her touch awakened a tingling along the length of his arm. Trying to ignore her effect on him, Marco kept up with her. What had she asked him? He frowned over the name. "He sounds familiar."

"He was on the football team for two years—"

"Oh."

The way he said "oh" irritated her. "He's not the stereotypical jock. He was on the honor roll all through college and has gone into corporate law. He's done quite well."

"Oh."

Stubborn man. But the joy of seeing Mimi again carried Spring along.

"What did she mean," Marco asked, "she's already got the ball rolling?"

"What do you think? Why are you here?" She shook her head at him as she topped the gangplank. A ship's photographer, dressed in crisp white, motioned them to pause. ''I've already called everyone who might be helpful, and the clinic is already a topic.''

Marco gawked at her.

The photographer snapped their photo.

Chapter Ten

As Spring and Marco in swimwear walked to the pool area on an upper deck, the hot Gulf sun beat down on her bare shoulders. The cloudless blue sky stretched above and the turquoise Gulf of Mexico rippled all around. White seagulls wheeled and squawked overhead. The ship had cast off early in the afternoon, and she was living her dream—she and Marco together.

Still, she trembled inside.

Marco continued his impersonation of a grumpy bear—a grumpy bear in new navy swim trunks. Why had her calling people and starting the talk about Marco's proposed free clinic upset him so? Did he intend to counter her every move, or would he cooperate?

She closed her eyes, again tapping into God's peace and asking for blessing. *Let me know Your will, God. If I'm supposed to be with Marco, let it become*

*plain to both of us. If the free clinic is in Your plan,
let us find contributors easily. I'm only human. I want
what I want. But Your will be done.*

She drew in a deep breath. "There are a pair of
lounge chairs." She headed toward the two, side by
side by the pool.

Marco trailed after her like a robot, no expression,
no comments. He could ruin everything! How could
she shake him out of his dour mood?

She eased down onto one wooden lounge chair and
Marco claimed the other. He let the back of it down
slightly to recline, folded his arms and closed his
eyes, as forbidding a pose as she could have imagined. Was he pouting or just oblivious to how to attract people in an engaging manner? Spring wanted
to shake him!

Even if he didn't feel like giving her any attention,
he had to look approachable, smile and talk to people.
Doing his impression of Ebenezer Scrooge wouldn't
win him any friends or contributors. She had to loosen
him up and do it without anyone noticing. She'd
never had to do anything like this before. How did
one get a man to laugh? Her mind brought up the
picture of her youngest sister surrounded by a circle
of jovial young men. How would Doree handle this
situation? That was easy. Doree always did the unexpected.

After a moment's consideration, Spring reached
into her beach bag and pulled out her sunscreen lotion. She mustered her courage and brooked no cow-
ardice. Still aghast at what she was about to do, she

rose and perched on the edge of Marco's lounger, forcing him to make room for her.

His eyes flew open.

"I know you probably won't burn—" she kept her tone light "—but I will. Would you put sunscreen on my back, please?"

He stared at her as if she was speaking Swahili.

Her nerves jiggling like soft-set gelatin, she shoved the tube into his hand, lifted her long hair and turned her back to him. *Get with the program, Marco!*

She waited. Finally, he snapped open the tube and she felt his firm hand on her back. The lotion felt cool, but her already sun-warmed back heated up as if it were blushing. Could backs blush?

"Be sure to put a thick coat on or I'll burn," she murmured from under her hair, as though men applied lotion to her back every day. She tried to reel in her reaction to his touch, but the task proved hopeless. Marco's touch was lovely. "Put a good coat on my shoulders, too."

Marco paused, then followed her instructions.

"Hey! That looks like hard work. Need any help?"

Spring thought she recognized the man's voice. Still holding her hair over her face, she looked up sideways. Yes, it was unfortunately the person she had thought it was. "Marco's doing just fine, Pete. No need to help."

Pete grinned with mischief in his eyes. "You missed a spot. Is it, Marco?" Pete offered his hand.

Marco paused just long enough to make Spring worry. Would he make polite conversation or be brusque? But after rubbing the excess lotion onto his muscled thigh, Marco took Pete's hand and shook it. "Marco Da Palma."

"Peter Rasmussen, Class of '91."

"Class of '89," Marco responded.

"Yeah, I thought you looked familiar. About time Spring dragged someone along with her. You'd think she'd have better luck getting dates—*Oof!*"

Spring had stopped his teasing with a punch to his middle. "You're getting soft, Pete. Maybe a few laps in the pool will get you back into shape."

Pete raised both hands in mock surrender. "Touchy, touchy."

Spring straightened, letting her hair fall over one shoulder. Marco handed her the tube. She motioned Marco to turn his back to her.

He stared at her without moving.

Doree never took no for an answer, so Spring quickly turned his shoulders the way she wanted them and applied a quick coat to Marco's shoulders and the back of his neck, the areas that her father always sunburned.

As though still unsettled, Marco cleared his throat. "What line of work are you into now, Pete?"

Spring wiped the leftover cream on Marco's nose, then moved back to her own lounger, breathing a silent sigh of relief.

"I've moved back to Florida and have just opened a law practice with another alumnus, Greg Fortney. Did you know him?"

"The name sounds familiar," Marco admitted.

"He graduated with your class." Pete called out, "Hey, Greg, come on over and meet Marco, the lucky man who came with Spring."

"Spring?" A tall lanky man stood up and walked over. "Not Spring Kirkland, the Snow Maiden?"

Spring hated the nickname she'd been given at college. But she tried hard to look as if she didn't care. Otherwise, Greg and Pete would tease her mercilessly.

Marco shook hands more firmly than he usually did with Greg. He'd heard Spring called this sobriquet, the Snow Maiden, at college. He hadn't liked it then. He liked it less now. But he took his cue from Spring. She was smiling at Greg, so Marco went along. *Just don't say anything else "cute," Greg.*

"What are you doing for a living, Marco?" Pete asked.

"I'm in private practice in Gulfview Shores."

"Law?" Greg asked.

"Family medicine."

For the next few minutes, Greg and Pete grilled him about med school and told a few law school stories. Marco tried to look interested, but so far they hadn't said anything he'd taken time off to board a ship to hear.

"Limbo break!" a feminine voice proclaimed.

Pete and Greg joined in the general shouting of approval. Before Marco could bow out, he'd been towed into line with most of the people who'd been lounging around the pool. He glanced around for an escape route.

"This will give us an appetite for dinner tonight!" Pete announced.

Spring turned back to Marco and murmured, "Would you rather not? It's always a lot of fun."

Her enchanting expression, a mixture of hope and doubt, made it impossible for him to refuse. He smiled for her benefit. "I don't think I've ever limboed before."

She chuckled. "I never last long, but watching the last few squeeze under is hilarious."

"Okay." He'd take his turn, fail, then just become an onlooker.

One of the cruise's social directors, a tall brunette in a yellow bikini and a dangerous-looking tan (hadn't anyone warned her about skin cancer?), stood by the stick that would be lowered inch by inch, and named the prizes for the person who could bend backward the lowest. The distinctive melody for the dance boomed out. Marco hadn't noticed the many speakers around the lounging area until then.

Pete started the chant. "Limbo! Limbo!" Soon it competed with the blasting, raucous music.

Lithe and graceful, Spring moved along in front of Marco. He had a hard time keeping his mind on the dance. He didn't want to stare at her. It would embarrass her. Fortunately, she'd chosen a discreet one-piece suit in a bold blue. If she'd selected one of the brief bikinis some of the other female alumni sported, he'd have been forced to feign seasickness and go back to his cabin.

Spring's turn came. The pole was at chin height,

so she slipped under it easily. Marco followed her and made certain he didn't disturb the pole by accident. If he messed up too early, it would make him even more noticed.

Pete and Greg hot-dogged under the pole amid laughter. The bouncy melody played on as the line made another circuit, another, another. Bumping the pole off its supports, Spring laughed at herself, then clapped in time with the music.

Caught up in the rhythm and gaiety, Marco bent backward and eased himself under the pole. By now, the line of contenders had thinned to less than a dozen.

When the pole touched Marco's waist, he decided he could blunder now and disappear into the crowd. He bent backward and began inching under the pole—

"Hey, Snow Maiden," Greg called from behind Marco. "Bet I can outdo your boyfriend!"

Marco gritted his teeth. *Not on a bet, Greg!* The pole grazed his navel—

Pete catcalled, "You're gonna lose it, Marco boy!"

Marco bent back and shuffled his feet forward inch by inch…then he was on the other side! Cheers went up.

Marco's face blazed with exhilaration and the unaccustomed experience of being the recipient of applause.

Spring patted his arm in approval.

Marco suffered her touch—sweet agony.

She started another chant. "Marco! Marco!"

The limbo melody played on. One by one, the remaining dancers were eliminated. Finally, only Pete, Greg and Marco competed for the prize. Giving in to defeat, Pete leaped over the pole, which now came knee-high to him. Greg grunted and bent backward, moving forward. He nearly made it, but his incipient paunch did him in. The pole clattered to the ship's deck.

Marco faced the pole. Should he just quit and let the prize go to the last person who'd made it through? A glance at Spring's hopeful face routed this idea.

Everyone fell silent as he flexed his knees as low as he could, bent his shoulders back as far as they would go, then began to bounce forward on his feet. The pole passed over his knees, his thighs, his navel, his chest—then he faced his greatest obstacle, his chin. Closing his eyes, he extended his neck back as low as it could go. He bounced forward, the silence around him suffocating. The pole shaved his nose, then skimmed his forehead— He cleared it!

The result was bedlam.

He stood up, blinking.

"You did it! You won!" Spring threw her arms around his neck.

In a natural reflex, he wrapped his arms around her. A ship's photographer snapped a victory photo of them. Pete and Greg thumped him on the back, shouting their congratulations.

Marco could hardly breathe. The combination of being the center of attention for the first time in his life and the sweet sensation of Spring in his arms swept away any conscious reactions.

"This is going to be fun!" Mimi shrilled in Marco's ear, or just below his ear. The four of them— Mimi and her husband, John, Spring and him—had just disembarked from the cruise ship onto the wharf of an island stop. The tropical sun blazed down on them, glinting off anything chrome or metal.

Spring's old college roommate, Mimi, didn't even come to Marco's shoulder. Her bubbly personality had irritated him at first when John and Mimi had joined them for dinner the night before. But Mimi had proved a delightful companion, funny and sweet. John appeared to stand back and enjoy his wife's easy charm. Marco had felt accepted and drawn into the good company in a way he'd never before experienced. He tried to analyze it but couldn't.

Now he gave Mimi a smile, then glanced to Spring. Her face glowed with her excitement as they put distance between themselves and the ship.

"I want to find something totally outrageous for my sister Doree's birthday," she said.

"Is she still in Madison at the university?" Mimi tugged at John's hand.

"Yes, she's a sophomore." Spring pulled at Marco's hand, too.

"What's the hurry?" Marco asked, enjoying the vacation-happy Spring beside him. "We've got the whole morning."

"It might take all morning to find something outrageous enough for my sister!"

Marco felt a twinge of conscience. He really didn't know much about Spring's family—just that her father was a pastor and they weren't rich. "Do you have any other siblings?" he murmured for her ears only.

She gave him a startled look. "Just Hannah, the food writer."

He grimaced. "Now I remember. You were telling Paloma about her on the way to Mamacita's."

She gave him a dazzling smile. "You remember that?"

He nodded, feeling guilty he'd made her remind him.

"Maybe you should find something for Paloma?" Spring suggested with an uncertain expression.

"You're right. She'd love something from here." *Why didn't I think of that?* Spring's constant thoughtfulness touched him. What a gentle heart she had.

He glanced around at the island thoroughfare they had just started down. Tropical shades of peach, pink, turquoise, tan and yellow decorated the tourist street on the island. Venders roamed along the street hawking their wares—straw hats, colorful stuffed animals, parrots, fresh flowers in bunches. Little open-air shops touted postcards, huge fun sunglasses, dried starfish and sea horses, and seashells.

"Will you help me find something for Paloma?"

"Of course."

When Spring took his hand, it seemed natural. Being away from their family and the town where he practiced medicine had stripped him of his reticence. He felt like a different man from the one who spent his days walking hospital hallways. Spring had been right to insist he come.

A break once in a while could be more than beneficial. Now her soft hand in his filled him with a wonder he could hardly process. *I'm holding hands with Spring and we're on a tropical island.*

After browsing in a series of crowded tourist shops, Marco chose a colorful toy parrot for Paloma, then dropped back behind the ladies with John, as their foursome went from store to store.

John, at his side, gave him a friendly grin. "Hope you're wearing comfortable shoes."

Marco lifted an eyebrow.

"We may end up walking up and down every street on this island. Mimi never stops shopping *till she drops.*" John gave his wife a loving glance.

Daunted by this remark, Marco looked down the long street of shops.

Glancing around, John halted when he saw Mimi go into yet another one. "How about we stay out here and have something to drink and wait for the ladies?" John motioned toward an open-air café on the opposite side of the dusty street.

"Sure." After calling their intentions to Spring and Mimi, Marco followed John to a table shaded by a woven canopy. They ordered chilled mineral water and sat back. The cadence of happy voices, reggae music in the distance, the brilliance of the sunshine— all combined to make a tranquil setting.

Marco sucked in a long cooling draught. He couldn't remember feeling so relaxed. ''I hadn't expected to enjoy myself.'' The words slipped out before he took time to consider each syllable the way he usually did. What would John think?

''Yeah, there's nothing like a cruise with old and new friends.'' He lifted his bottle to Marco. ''I wouldn't take the time to do this kind of stuff, but Mimi always keeps tabs on what's going on and when I need a vacation.''

''You're lucky.'' And Marco meant it.

John chuckled. ''And you're the envy of half the guys on the cruise. I can't believe Spring still isn't married.''

Marco stiffened, but he could read no ulterior message in John's face, his easy smile. ''Spring is a very special lady.''

''You'll get no argument from me.'' John swallowed the rest of his water and motioned for another. ''I hear you're trying to raise funds for a free clinic.''

Marco searched John's expression and began tentatively. ''Yes, I'd like to be able to offer emergency and short-term care for people who don't have medical coverage, for whatever reason.''

''Mimi says you've got a site chosen?''

Instead of tensing up as he had when Spring had first discussed his asking for contributions, the words, the plans flowed from Marco. John sounded interested and asked intelligent questions. One, then two, then three other guys from the cruise, including Pete and Greg, stopped by and joined in the discussion.

Marco absorbed the camaraderie, something he'd rarely experienced before. He seldom attended the hospital's social functions. Why was he accepted now, when he hadn't been in college?

He looked up to find Spring standing just outside the café watching him. Everyone seemed to accept Spring and him as a couple. The fact had astounded him at first, but the idea was becoming more agreeable hour by hour. He waved.

She smiled.

Tenderness for her flowed warm inside him. *Spring, is it possible? Do I have a chance with you?*

The ice sculptures glistened in the low light of the ship's large dining room. Spring sat at an oblong table beside Marco. The dinner buffet—succulent prime rib, Cornish hen, duck, lobster and King crab—had been sumptuous, as usual. She'd eaten more on this cruise than she had ever eaten before! The waist of her pale pink evening gown circled her a bit tighter than it had last year.

Tonight was the last night of the cruise. The thought saddened her. Would the special closeness she and Marco had shared here disappear when they returned to Gulfview Shores?

The cruise had been all she'd hoped for and more. Marco had relaxed and he'd begun to behave differently—as if he had finally noticed that she was a woman. Did she have a chance with Marco, after all this time? Tomorrow morning when she stepped down from the gangplank, would she turn back into a disenchanted Cinderella?

The live band struck up another romantic ballad. John took Mimi by the hand and led her to the dance floor. Soon every other couple at their table had moved onto the dance floor or to other tables to chat.

Marco looked to her. "Would you like to dance?"

"You dance?"

He grinned. "Paloma taught me for a hospital benefit."

Unable to trust her voice at the thought of being held in Marco's strong arms, she nodded.

He took her hand and led her through the maze of tables to join the other couples. Then he faced her, and his hand settled on the small of her back.

Thrilled at this dream-come-true intimacy, she rested one hand on his broad shoulder and clasped his hand in the other. In the dim light, she focused on his dark intense eyes and the feel of being so near the man she loved. She closed her eyes then and let herself revel in his embrace.

Marco felt as though his heart were being drawn from his chest. Her fragrance of gardenias, the low lighting, the mellow music, the soft form in his arms intoxicated him more powerfully than any wine he could have sipped. *Spring Kirkland in my arms.* The melody carried him on, dreamlike.

He thought of Spring's gentle care of *Tía* Rosita, her sympathy toward Paloma in the vice-principal's office, her enthusiasm for his free clinic. Most men only noticed the lovely package Spring came in, but her kind, generous heart had proved even more exceptional.

The dance ended.

Spring gazed up at him, her eyes glowing with tenderness.

For him? What could she see in him?

"Let's go outside and walk the deck in the moonlight," she murmured.

He nodded, unable to speak.

She took his arm.

Brushing past other couples, he piloted her through the crowded room, then out onto the deck. The warm night breeze caressed his face. He led her away to a quiet spot. A phrase came to his mind so inadequate to the moment, but he voiced it anyway. "It's a beautiful night."

His low, husky voice made prickles run up Spring's arms.

"I hate to see the cruise end." She moved closer to him.

"I feel the same way."

Bliss romped inside her. She'd never thought she'd hear him say those words. Could he be changing? "We didn't find any backers—"

He pressed his hand to her lips, stopping her words. "We tried. We did our best. Let's just enjoy our last night on board."

She nodded, holding back happy tears. Marco didn't even sound like the same man who'd called the cruise a "waste of time."

Marco didn't feel like himself at all. The blond lady

in the pink evening gown beside him shimmered in the moonlight like molten Black Hills gold—irresistible. He took a step closer.

She leaned forward.

He bent his head.

She lifted her face.

His lips touched hers. *Spring*...

"Hey! Marco!" Pete's now familiar voice rocketed through Marco. His hands balled into fists. He turned to face Pete.

Pete grinned at him. "Sorry to interrupt, old man. But I think we need to talk. Greg and I want to back that clinic of yours."

Chapter Eleven

Had it all happened? Marco still felt a little light-headed. Lavender twilight hugged the Gulf as he opened the door of his car to let Spring into the front passenger seat.

When she glanced up, he nearly lost himself in the shadowed blue of her lovely eyes. *Qué bella es.*

Spring sighed. "I'm glad you're driving me home. I still feel a little unsteady—the ship and so much happening...."

He understood the hesitance in her voice. He was experiencing the same kind of disorientation. He'd come home a different man. How could so much occur in three short—change that to very *long*—days? He'd gone on the cruise just to get everyone off his back. He hadn't expected it to be so...what? He tried to process all that had happened, all that had shifted, changed.

Chaotic inside, he settled himself beside Spring and

backed his car out of the parking space. "Do you think they were serious?"

"Yes. Pete can be irritating, always the clown, but evidently he has a serious side. I can't believe he would tell you something he didn't mean to do."

"I guess you're right. I just never imagined..." He shrugged his shoulders. *I never imagined just how much I wanted to be close to you.*

Spring turned to him with a smile. "Never ask God for something and expect nothing."

Her glowing face warmed his blood. Still, he couldn't just let her statement stand. "But prayers aren't always answered."

"Yes, they are. People only want a firm 'yes'— usually by way of an eye-opening miracle. They think that's God's one and only way of answering prayer. But God answers prayers in many ways and He gives *every* prayer one of three possible answers."

"And what are these three?"

"They are Yes, No, Wait. We humans prefer yes and tend to dislike the negative and patience answers."

"I must be accustomed to the latter two. I'm stunned. I admit it. I never expected to find donors, not big ones. And certainly not Pete and Greg." When Pete had interrupted his near kissing of Spring, Marco had wanted to deck him. The raw anger he'd felt came back. But it gave way to wonder. *Spring, you were ready to let me kiss you.*

She grinned, as though reading his mind. "'Be

careful what you pray for, you might get it' is another favorite saying of my mother's."

He snorted. "She's got something there."

Spring swirled toward him on the car seat. "Aren't you happy? Isn't this wonderful? Pete and Greg will give you the whole down payment for the church—"

"*If* I can get nonprofit status." There was always at least one more hurdle to jump, in his life.

She waved this objection away with one hand. "They even said they'd draw up the nonprofit status papers for you to sign. Why would the state of Florida deny a free clinic nonprofit status?"

"I don't know, but I never take any challenge for granted." His voice roughened. One's own hard work was the only thing one could count on.

"I have faith in Pete and Greg, in the state of Florida, in God and in *you*, Marco Da Palma." She faced forward again.

Don't turn away. "I didn't mean to offend you."

"You didn't. I just get the feeling that you don't know how to trust God in every situation."

Did Spring have that kind of faith? "Do you?" he asked.

"It depends," she replied. "I try to. I think my parents do. It isn't easy. I usually want to stick an oar in and help God. That's what Aunt Geneva always says."

He gave a sardonic grin. "I believe that."

The sweet woman beside him giggled.

He threaded his way through the darkened streets of Gulfview to her aunt's house. As he drove through the quieter residential streets, he watched emotion play over Spring's expressive face. *Do you want to be close to me too, Spring? Is that possible?*

Too soon he turned down her street. The early March sun had just dipped below the horizon casting its last golden rays, when he pulled up to her house. He helped her out, then carried her two bags to the door.

"It's been a long day."

"Yes, that engine problem slowed down our trip back to port, but I enjoyed the extra hours on deck. See?" She held out her arm toward him. "I'm almost golden."

Golden. Precious. Radiant. These words describing Spring wended through his mind. He wished for the music of the night before, so he could hold her in his arms again. He took her soft hand, hating to be parted.

She looked up at him expectantly.

"Spring, I...the cruise...everything." He struggled for words. "Our weekend was great. And I didn't expect it to be anything like it turned out."

She grinned at him. "I know. You made that clear. But I saw you mellow."

Her smile turned his heart inside out. Tugging on her hand, he pulled her into his arms.

A little gasp of surprise escaped her.

He waited. Would she pull away?

She leaned into his embrace.

Exultant, he tightened his grasp on her. "Spring, you're so lovely, so good...I..." He kissed her.

"Marco," she murmured against his lips as she twined her arms around his neck.

Marco immersed himself in the sensations Spring's kiss released within him. Strength surged through him and possessiveness made him draw her more tightly to him.

Spring lost the feeling of separateness between Marco and herself. His warm skin under her lips and his strong arms banded around her. She clung to him, not trusting her own strength.

At last, the delicious, thrilling kiss ended.

She stared up at him, dazed. She breathed out his name. "Marco."

"Mi querida," he whispered against her cheek.

She didn't know the exact translation of his words, but she loved the way he said it with such emotion, such restrained passion. She smiled up at him.

He loosened his hold on her, bit by bit, as though bringing them both gently back to earth. "I should be going. It's late," he apologized, then released her completely.

She immediately folded her arms in front of her, bereft. "I know. Good night."

"Buenas noches, Señorita." He touched her cheek, then moved away.

Waving, she watched him walk back to his car. She didn't go in until his car drove out of sight. Then turning, she opened the door.

"That was so romantic!" Matilde exclaimed, her hands clasped together.

"Oh, Spring, darling," Aunty declared, "the cruise must have been a success! He kissed you!"

"You two have got to stop spying on me!" Spring protested. Chagrin cut through her, fiery heat burning her cheeks. Even in her anger, though, she realized their spying came from affection.

The two older women had the honesty to blush.

"We didn't mean anything bad," Matilde rushed to assure her.

"Of course not," Aunty agreed, and bowed her head contritely for a moment.

Spring shook her head at them. She didn't begrudge them the joy of seeing what they'd hoped for, but knowing that she and Marco hadn't been truly alone in that special moment did cause some of its power to evaporate.

"We'll never do it again—" Aunty began.

"We never thought he would kiss you." Matilde sighed. "And such a kiss, too. My heart melts when I remember..." Matilde's voice stopped and she blushed a deeper rosy pink.

"I remember, too," Aunty said. "A rumble seat. His name was Floyd, but I thought he was the nearest thing to Rudolph Valentino I'd ever see." She sighed, then grimaced. "My jaw keeps aching. I was just to the dentist before you came, Spring. Ooh. I'm falling apart daily." Aunty pressed her hand to her jaw.

"Your jaw, your arm. Do you want me to get your liniment?" Matilde asked with obvious concern.

"No, I'll be fine." But her aunt's expression belied her short words.

Matilde shook her finger at Aunty. "You worked too hard today in the garden—"

"Stop scolding, Matilde." Aunty grimaced. " A couple of aspirin and I'll be fine. Now go to bed."

Shaking her head at their bickering, Spring picked up her handbag and rolled her wheeled suitcase down the hallway. "Come on. I'll tell you what happened on the cruise."

"Did Marco have luck getting backers?" Matilde called after her.

"Yes, he—"

"No, don't tell me! I want to be able to hear all about it from his mother. You two go ahead. I'm sleepy. *Buenas noches!*"

"Don't tell her Marco kissed me!" Spring begged her.

"No, no, I won't!" Matilde promised.

Spring and Aunty waved good-night to Matilde and walked into Spring's room. Aunty went straight to the bedside chair as though the short walk had drained her. Uneasy, Spring sank down on the bed.

"So Marco found contributors?" Aunty rubbed her arm.

Spring began watching her aunt closely, but replied, "Yes, two alumni who just opened their own law practice north of here in Sarasota. They just won a big case and wanted to tithe their earnings."

"Wonderful!"

"Yes, it's enough for the down payment on the church.... Aunty, is your arm troubling you?"

"Yes, Matilde is right. I must have done too much

gardening this afternoon, though I didn't think I did any more than usual—''

Spring leaned over and took one of her aunt's hands in hers. What she saw sent her reeling. ''Aunty! Your fingernails are turning blue.''

Aunt Geneva glanced down. ''So they are. How peculiar.''

Spring reached for the phone and dialed, her pulse racing with alarm.

''Who are you calling?''

''Marco's cell phone number.'' Now she wished he'd stayed and come in with her.

''Why?''

''Because…'' She held up her hand when the phone was picked up. ''Marco, my aunt's jaw is aching. Her arm is giving her pain and her fingernails are turning blue. Should I be concern— Yes, okay. I will. Thanks.'' She hung up and dialed again, sick with apprehension.

''What's the matter?'' Aunt Geneva asked, sitting forward.

''He said to call 911.'' She kept her tone neutral. ''He thinks you're close to a heart attack.''

''But—''

''Hello, this is Spring Kirkland at 677 Mimosa Lane. My aunt, Mrs. Geneva Dorfman, needs an ambulance. Her doctor told me to call. She may be near cardiac arrest. Yes. Thank you.'' Spring hung up the phone.

''I'm not having a heart attack! I just strained my

arm.'' Her aunt's face crumbled. ''I...oh, oh, my chest...I...''

''Don't try to talk.'' Again, Spring kept panic out of her tone. ''They'll be here right away. Don't worry.'' She ran to the door, opened it and called, ''Matilde! Matilde!''

Spring held her aunt's limp hand in the brightly lit emergency room cubicle. Just outside the door, Matilde sat, her eyes closed, her lips moving in prayer. As Spring had driven them to the hospital following the ambulance, she had feared the housekeeper would have a heart attack herself.

At the hospital, after complaining about a feeling of heavy weight on her chest, Aunty lost consciousness. Now her aunt's mouth and nose were covered with an oxygen mask, and an IV had been inserted in one arm. She looked pale, sickly pale. Her fingernails were much bluer than when Spring first had examined them at home.

Marco, please come. Marco! Dear Lord, please take care of Aunty, please take care. Her mind alternated between these two pleas. Spring fiercely held tears at bay.

A doctor, a stranger to Spring, hovered around Aunt Geneva. ''How long had your aunt been experiencing arm pain?''

''She didn't say. I'd just come home from a weekend away—''

Marco strode into the room. ''Dr. Hansen!''

Spring's heart lurched in her chest. She rose from her chair but retained her aunt's hands.

"Dr. Da Palma, Mrs. Dorfman is your patient?"

"Yes, what have you done?"

Dr. Hansen handed him the chart. "The usual. I've had blood drawn, started an ECG, and ordered a *stat* chest X ray."

Spring heard the words, but didn't really understand them. She watched Marco's face, trying to read it.

Marco nodded and thanked the doctor. He turned to Spring. "I'm glad you called me. When did your aunt lose consciousness?"

"Just after we arrived here," Spring replied.

A nurse came for Dr. Hansen. He excused himself and left with her.

Spring let go of her aunt's hand and took a step forward. Marco came to her and wrapped his arms around her. She melted against him, seeking his strength. Just last week she'd never have sought his embrace so naturally. What a difference three days had made.

"Is she going to be all right?"

"For now." He kissed her forehead. "Dr. Hansen and the EMTs appear to have her stabilized, and the right tests have been ordered."

The touch of his lips fortified her, even as she glanced back at her aunt.

Matilde stood up and came to the doorway. "Marco, why is she unconscious?"

He turned his head toward her. "A heart malfunctioning can be painful. She may have fainted because of that. Or lack of oxygen in the blood. She's being given morphine, which would take away the pain but make her groggy. She's definitely in distress, but she's here in the hospital. She'll get the best care possible.''

Spring rested her head on his chest, so comforting, so strong. She spoke words straight from her heart. "I'm so glad you're here."

He tucked her closer to him. "I'm glad you were there. You picked up on the symptoms of impending heart failure exactly. How did you know?"

"My father has had a few bouts with arrhythmia."

Marco tightened his hold on her.

"Isn't there anything else we can do?" She glanced into his deep brown eyes.

"No, *mi querida,* we'll watch her closely and make decisions about what is to be done. I'm going to call the staff's heart specialist. He'll read the tests, and we'll consult together."

A man in a lab coat entered the room. "I'm here to do Mrs. Dorfman's chest X ray."

Marco nodded, then led Spring from the room.

She glanced back at Aunty. The electrodes applied to Aunty's chest, the oxygen monitor on her index finger, the IV in her arm—everything made her aunt look so strange, so alone, so ill. Spring swallowed tears. *Dear Lord, help the staff here do what is best for my aunt. I love her so.*

About an hour later, a nurse moved Aunt Geneva upstairs to the cardiac intensive care unit, and Spring followed her. Aunty woke for a moment but was too weak to speak. Spring pressed her aunt's hand in both of hers. "You'll be all right, Aunty. Marco is here and everything is going as it should."

Her aunt nodded slightly, then closed her eyes.

Marco drew Spring from the room with him. "You'll be allowed in only fifteen minutes every hour. We'll go sit in the lounge area on this floor."

Spring objected. "You have to work in the morning. You might have to assist in surgery for Aunty. You need your rest."

"I'll be fine."

When she tried to object further, he pressed his hand to her lips. She conceded.

He led Matilde and her to a comfortable lounge area just down the hall. He helped Matilde settle into an arm chair. "Try to rest."

Matilde wiped tears from her eyes. "She's such a good woman." She clutched Marco's arm.

"She's getting the best care available and she's a strong woman." Marco covered Matilde's hand with his.

"You are right. She came through a war. She survived losing the man she loved twenty years ago." Matilde took a deep breath. "I will pray and have faith."

Marco nodded and patted Matilde's shoulder. He motioned Spring to sit on a cushy sofa, then sat down beside her.

His presence made all the difference to her. Marco

wouldn't let Aunty receive anything but the best treatment. She gave him a tremulous smile.

She noticed a beige phone on the table beside her, with printed instructions on how to dial an outside local line. More prayers could only help. She opened her purse and pulled out her phone calling card, picked up the receiver and dialed.

"Mother, it's Spring. I called for prayer support. Aunty's in intensive care...."

Chapter Twelve

Stiff, Spring sat up and stretched. Instantly, concern for her aunt balled tight in her stomach, making her feel nauseated. She hadn't left the hospital all night. Aunt Geneva had slept fitfully, but had finally stabilized. Still in cardiac intensive care, she was far from well.

Slumped back in the corner of the armchair, Matilde looked up, groggy. "What's happening?"

Spring glanced at her watch and stood up carefully, unsure of her legs after a night of on-and-off sleeping, sitting up and pacing. With both hands, she tried to brush the wrinkles from her skirt. "Marco and the heart specialist are to meet at seven this morning to make a decision about Aunty and heart surgery. It's about that now."

Matilde pushed herself up, stretching, too. "Oh, I need a cup of coffee—"

"*Hola!*" Anita bustled off the elevator toward

them. "I'm so glad you called me, Matilde. As soon as I made breakfast for Santos and Paloma, I came right over. You should go home and get some rest." Anita gathered Spring into her arms for an affectionate hug, much to Spring's surprise.

Spring breathed in the mingled fragrances of Anita's sweet perfume and fresh bacon—homey aromas, so welcome in this clinical setting. "I didn't know Matilde had called you."

"You were napping. I called about an hour ago. I know Santos always rises early."

Spring didn't know what to say. She'd never expected Marco's mother to come.

"I know we've just met," Anita said. "But I feel like I know you and your aunt from all Matilde has told us about you over the years."

"It's very thoughtful of you."

"Señora Dorfman is a good woman, and you're Paloma and Marco's friend." Anita smiled.

Spring's mind a jumble of thoughts, she urged Anita to sit down beside her, then filled her in on her aunt's night and what was going to be done for Aunty this morning.

Marco strode up the hall toward them.

Rising, Spring met him and held out her hands. She craved his reassuring touch.

He gripped them and pulled her a step closer. "I discussed your aunt with Dr. Carlson, the heart specialist on staff."

Spring nodded, unable to think of anything to say. ECGs, ICUs, and IVs weren't a part of her everyday life. His nearness bolstered her. She longed to tell him so, but couldn't with his mother looking on.

Marco glanced past Spring. "Mother, you're here."

"*Sí*, Matilde called me. I thought Spring could use some more support."

Anita looked as though she were challenging Marco in some way Spring couldn't understand.

But Marco only nodded again, then turned back to Spring. "Dr. Carlson has ordered immediate surgery for your aunt. A double bypass."

Spring's knees weakened. She slipped back down to the sofa. "Then Aunty's condition is as serious as I feared."

Marco didn't let go of her hands. He sat down beside her. "Carlson is the best. I'm going to scrub to assist him. The good news is that your aunt's heart hasn't had previous damage and the bypass will bring her back to health."

"It's all happening so suddenly…." Spring's voice faltered.

Matilde began crying again.

"We're very lucky. Dr. Carlson had planned to take off today so he has time to do her surgery."

Spring pursed her lips. "I know you'll do what's best."

Then he surprised her by kissing her forehead. What would his mother think?

He stood. "Matilde, would you please take Spring down to the cafeteria and make sure she eats a good breakfast?"

Spring turned pink at his proprietary tone. Did he hear how he sounded? "No, I couldn't—"

Matilde cut in. *"Claro que sí."* She took one of Spring's hands. "Help me, Anita. This girl eats like a bird."

Marco let Spring's other hand drop, then leaned forward to kiss her. This time lightly on her lips. "Go. You need to eat."

His kiss ran through her like warm maple syrup, sweet and delicious, in spite of his mother's presence. Spring gazed into his eyes, reading his concern there. She nodded.

"Take your time eating breakfast. The surgery will take hours."

She watched him march away, longing to urge him to stay.

Anita excused herself to run a quick errand for Paloma, but promised to meet them in the surgical waiting area.

Downstairs, wandering down the cafeteria line, Spring selected tea and dry toast. Following behind, Matilde added fresh fruit and a bowl of oatmeal to Spring's tray.

A little queasy from lack of sleep, Spring frowned and tried to put both bowls back.

"No! You must eat to keep up your strength!" Matilde objected.

"I won't be able to eat—"

"You will." Matilde's chin rose stubbornly.

"But—"

The housekeeper sighed. "Eat what you can, *hija*

mia. You don't need to eat all of everything, just a bit of each. Toast and tea will not give you the strength you need now.''

Spring nodded but felt too nervous to eat. The appetite she'd acquired on the cruise had vanished, leaving her hollow.

She paid for her breakfast, and Matilde followed her to a table near the wall of windows overlooking the hospital garden. Pink azaleas festooned borders of white petunias in the bright sunshine. She bowed her head to give thanks. When she looked up, she still had no appetite.

The words she'd been holding in all night came rushing out. ''I feel so guilty.''

''Why?''

''I should have noticed Aunty wasn't feeling well.'' Spring felt her throat thicken with emotion. ''I shouldn't have gone away—''

''No!'' Matilde shook her head vigorously. ''She was thrilled for you. Marco and you going on that cruise made her so happy.''

Unable to speak, Spring forked a chunk of cantaloupe into her mouth. The fresh, cool fruit woke her taste buds and made her stomach clamor for more.

''Marco kissed you last night and this morning,'' Matilde murmured with a knowing smile. ''What happened on the cruise?''

Spring paused with her fork poised over the fruit. What a question. How could she put all that had occurred into words to be said over breakfast. ''Marco was able to get donors for his free clinic.''

"Wonderful, but what happened between you two?"

Spring speared a fresh, ripe strawberry. "I don't know. We're closer but we haven't talked."

"Ay!" Matilde struck her forehead. "You will give me a heart attack, too. You two need someone to teach you how to fall in love!"

On her way into surgery, Aunt Geneva clutched Spring's hands in hers, communicating her anxiety.

"You'll be all right, Aunty," Spring murmured. "Dr. Carlson is the best in Florida and Marco will be with him. You won't be in surgery so very long."

"Spring, I've been thinking." Aunty's eyes looked frightened and distracted. "I should have told you about your mother's natural parents. If I should die today…no one else knows the truth!"

"You can tell me after you're out of surgery." Spring said it with a hopeful smile, though she felt the drag of worry around her heart. *Oh, Lord, please protect my dear aunt.*

Aunty had been given something to relax her, but obviously it hadn't lessened her anxiety. Her eyes filled with tears. "But, Spring, I—"

The orderly apologized, but pushed the gurney the last few feet to the pre-operating room door.

Spring waved to her aunt and blew a kiss. She watched until her aunt was out of sight, then her tears let down like a sudden storm. Feeling unreasonably guilty for ever asking about her mother's adoption, she turned and made her way to the surgical waiting room.

"Spring!" Anita welcomed her with open arms. "*Pobrecita,* you poor child."

"I love her so much," Spring said, her words mangled by a sudden rush of weeping.

"She will be fine," Anita comforted her. "Matilde and I will stay with you until she is out of surgery and we know she is safe."

"We're here, too, Spring." Verna Rae came in with Eleanor at her side, just behind Anita.

Verna Rae continued. "Hon, our churches are all prayin' for your aunt."

"She's a strong one, that Geneva," Eleanor added. "Don't count her out, dahling. She's got a lot of years left in her!"

Fresh tears spilled from Spring's eyes, but gratitude curved her face into a reluctant smile. "I'm so glad Aunty has such good friends."

"And such a good doctor!" Eleanor finished for her. "Matilde introduced us to Dr. Da Palma's mother here. She's a sweetheart, too—"

"So you have nothing to worry about, honey." Verna Rae patted Spring's arm.

Spring nodded. "Thank you. I'm better now." She sat down, and each lady found a comfortable spot near her in the corner of the surgical waiting area. Her spirits had risen.

God, be there and watch over Aunt Geneva. I love her so. And bless the doctors who are operating. Be with Marco as he assists. I love him, Lord—even if I can't bring myself to say the words to him.

"Spring." A soft, deep voice murmured her name. "Spring."

Chills up her spine woke her completely. She looked up into Marco's dark eyes. "Marco." Warmth swirled through her. She stretched in the chair beside her aunt's bed in the cardiac wing.

He whispered, "You should go home and get some sleep in your own bed. You've been here most of the past two days. Dr. Carlson is not concerned about your aunt's recovery at all. You can't do anything for her, can you."

"I wish I could do something. I'd feel better, then." Marco's low voice awoke her mind, body and heart—his tender concern for her, a priceless gift in a frantic time. Disheveled, she felt disoriented, as though she'd been tossed in a blanket several times, then dropped on her head. She glanced to her aunt, who lay sound asleep in her bed nearby.

"I was here when she told you to go home and rest," Marco coaxed, leaning close.

Spring laid her hand against his stubbled cheek. The contact sent a charge up her numb arm. "It's late. Why are you still here?"

He exhaled deeply. "I had a few emergencies at the office, then I was called back here for some more. Now I'm going to head home for a shower and some real sleep."

"Sounds good."

"Up." He tugged her hands, pulling her onto her feet. "Your aunt told you to go home. I'm going to take you there."

His strength beckoned her. Her mood lightened. "I love it when you bully me." Her emotions bubbled up. She felt giddy—from fatigue, from relief over the successful surgery?

"You are overtired. Now come." He led her from her aunt's room.

Feeling light as fresh soap bubbles, Spring let him lead her. "You'll have to call me a cab—"

"I'll drive you home."

"My aunt's house is out of your way."

"No one but me will be driving you home," he informed her in a fierce voice.

His tone set off a ringing of joy inside her. She giggled. "You're so masterful, Marco."

He gave her a disgruntled look, but towed her closer to him.

She reveled in his nearness, his tender care. Soon fresh Gulf air flowed over Spring's face. The night was still new and she could hear the sounds of traffic on the nearby highway. She let Marco lead her to his car, tuck her inside and drive her away.

All that had happened over the past week had pulled her away from everyday life. Her restless emotions lay just beneath the surface, ready to leap up at any cause. She laid her head back against the seat. "You have a wonderful family. Anita and Santos have been so kind."

"*Gracias.* My mother felt you needed someone, some family with you."

His words comforted her. "That's just what it felt like. I can see now why you are such a good man."

"I'm just a man—"

"Your mother said you were already fourteen when she married Santos, so the credit must go to your father. He must have made a lasting impression on you," Spring probed gently. Would Marco open up and tell her more about his personal life?

Marco's throat tightened. "My father was the best."

She stroked his arm, wanting, needing to make contact with him. "I'm so sorry you lost him. He would be very proud of you. How did you lose him? Was it an illness?"

"No." His voice sounded, felt hoarse. "He was killed in a car accident on Highway 19."

"I'm so sorry."

Marco couldn't stop himself. Words he'd never said to anyone else slipped through his lips. "I was with him in the car. A drunk driver hit us head-on. I was safely in the back seat. My father died before the ambulance came. I felt so helpless…. That's when I decided to be a doctor. I never wanted to be helpless again—when someone I loved needed me."

She slid closer to him, wrapped her arms around his right arm and nestled her face into his starched cotton shirt. "How awful for you. I know how that feels."

"You do?"

She rubbed her face against his shirt as she nodded. "My mother was diagnosed with leukemia three years ago."

"I didn't know!" He kissed her hair. "How is she? What are they doing for her?"

She pressed herself closer to him. "She's in remission now, has been for over eighteen months, but it was so scary. We were so afraid that we might lose her."

He covered her hand with his. "I'm so glad to hear that she is doing well."

She touched her cheek to his hand. "We, my sisters and father and I, still worry. What if the leukemia comes back?"

He spoke with urgency. "There are many treatments. We have so many new ways to treat leukemia—bone marrow transplants—"

"My sisters and I weren't matches."

"How about other family members?" Concern resonated in his voice.

She shook her head. "Mother was adopted, and we don't know anything about her birth family connections."

"That's tough." Marco thought about his only having his mother here in Florida. The rest of his relatives had stayed in Santo Domingo. He'd thought he had so little in common with Spring, but perhaps he'd been wrong.

So conscious of the lovely woman pressed close to him, Marco stopped in front of her aunt's home. He turned to Spring. She came into his arms so naturally that it took his breath away.

He forced back all the negative cautions that percolated up from his mind. *I want to kiss her. She wants my kiss. We're not so different!*

She lifted her face to him.

He kissed her, then stroked the golden strands of hair away from her pale, lucent face. *I love you, Spring. Te amo. Where will my feelings take us? Could you love me, too?*

Three days later, Spring sat beside her aunt's hospital bed and smiled. "You look stronger today."

"I feel like a crushed lettuce leaf."

Spring chuckled and enjoyed the light feeling it gave her. The past five days had been overloaded with worry, heart-wringing prayer and lack of sleep. But, at last, she felt hopeful.

Aunt Geneva stared into Spring's eyes as though she had something important on her mind.

Spring didn't look away. She thought she knew what her aunt wanted to discuss. "Are you going to tell me about mother now?"

Aunty nodded.

Though excited to be this close to the truth, Spring hesitated. "Are you certain you're up to this? I don't want you to overdo."

"I'm strong enough to talk. I've prayed about this every waking hour since I knew I was to go into surgery. You shocked me so when you asked me— out of the blue—about Ethel's parents. I've suppressed what I knew for so many years. I've thought more than once in the past ten years that maybe Ethel should be told.''

Aunty paused to sigh. ''Times have changed. Adoption used to be so hush-hush. Children were never even told they'd been adopted! Fortunately, your grandmother didn't do that! When Ethel was twelve, Gloria told her that she'd been adopted, but that Gloria and Tom couldn't love her any more than her natural mother did. Which was the truth. Gloria and I and both our husbands adored Ethel from the very first time we saw her.''

''When was that?'' Spring asked softly. How had her mother felt when she'd learned about her adoption?

''It's a sad story. Ethel's mother was Connie Wilson, a dear girl who grew up just across the street from your grandmother and me. She was a bit younger than me and a bit older than Gloria.'' Aunty's face took on a faraway expression. ''So many years ago. So sad that Connie…left us so soon.''

This thought had already occurred to Spring. ''Connie died young?''

Aunty nodded. ''It was wartime, you know, World War II. Connie went to work in a munitions factory in Milwaukee. She met a sailor from Great Lakes Naval Base near Waukegan, Illinois. He'd taken the North Shore train to Milwaukee. They fell in love at first sight.'' A tear trickled down her aunt's soft, wrinkled cheek.

Sorry to have brought pain to Aunt Geneva, Spring

handed her a soft tissue from a box on her bedside tray. "They never married?"

Aunty dabbed her eyes. "Connie had an engagement ring and she was so happy. But it was 1945, no time to be in love. He shipped out and was killed in action."

The long-ago story still had the power to stir Spring to pity. *Poor Connie.*

"But my mother was born."

"Yes, I believe that he intended to marry Connie. In fact, he wanted to marry Connie before he left, but her parents persuaded her not to marry until he came home. He wasn't good enough for them!" Aunty's voice became fierce. "They shouldn't have meddled. They let Bill go off to war. Then Connie came up pregnant, and they didn't want anyone to know. But Connie told me and Gloria."

Aunty's face started to pick up color again as her agitation mounted. "Her parents should have kept her home with them! People in town knew what kind of girl Connie was! Everyone knew she and Bill were engaged, and in wartime these things happen. But they hushed everything up and sent their only daughter away to an aunt's to have the baby."

"I'm sure they did what they thought was best." *But I could never do that!*

Aunty pursed her lips. "I've always believed that Connie wouldn't have died if she'd been at home when she had her baby. Who knew what kind of doctor she had, what kind of care!"

Spring couldn't think of any reply to this, so she

returned to the reason she'd disturbed the past. "Did Connie have any brothers and sisters?"

"Only one brother. He died in the Battle of the Bulge." Aunty drew a long breath. "Such sad times to remember." She wiped away new tears.

Spring touched her aunt's arm. "What was Mother's father's name?"

"Bill Smith. But it's a dead end, Spring. He died when his ship was attacked in the Pacific. So you see, there isn't anyone—"

"Maybe he had brothers or sisters," Spring offered.

"He might have. It was so long ago, I've forgotten…if I ever knew that to start with. I can't give you much to work with to find out if he had any other family."

Aunty reached for Spring's hand. "But I wanted you to know. Your mother may want to know someday, and I might not be here to tell her the story." Aunty tried to smile. "Connie had a first cousin in Oconomowoc, too, but she may be dead or long gone by now. I only remember her first name, Mary Beth."

The sad story tugged at her heart, and Spring rose and kissed her aunt's cheek. "Thank you for telling me. We might never find any blood relatives and we might never need them. Mother's leukemia may never come back."

Aunty fussed with her blanket. "I just hope I've done right to tell you."

"Aunt Geneva, as you've said, times have changed. This should have been revealed years ago."

"You're probably right, dear. Connie wanted Gloria to take her baby. She knew Gloria had just married Tom and that they'd take good care of her.''

''Connie's parents didn't want their only grand-child?''

Aunty pursed her lips. ''Our mother always said they were too concerned about what people would say. Their loss. Ethel was welcomed into our family with open arms.''

''Did Grandmother choose the name Ethel?''

''No, Connie named her.''

''I wonder why she chose that name.''

''I don't know. I'm sorry, dear, but I'm tired now.''

''I'm sure you are. Close your eyes. I'm going down to the cafeteria and get something to eat.''

''You do that, dear. I'm afraid you've lost weight again.''

Spring grinned. ''Not a bit. I gained weight on the cruise, and Matilde has had me under surveillance. I have not gone hungry!''

''Soon I want to hear all about the cruise!''

''Soon,'' Spring promised. She walked out into the hallway.

What would her sisters, Hannah and Doree, have to say about this? Was there any chance of finding blood relatives? The story didn't seem to give them much in the way of leads.

Is that Your answer, Lord? Are we to leave this all in Your hands and quit meddling, too?

''All right. Are we all on the line?'' Spring asked over the phone, sitting on her bed at Aunt Geneva's house later that evening.

"I'm here," Hannah replied.

"Me, too!" Doree exclaimed. "So what's the deal? Did Aunt Geneva give you the scoop?"

Spring sighed. "Aunty is much better this evening. Thank you for asking."

"Of course she is!" Doree declared. "Mom called me last night and told me that—"

Hannah interrupted, "I think Spring is trying to teach you how to begin a phone conversation. Certainly *someone* needs to do that. Aunty just had serious surgery after having had a heart attack—you should ask about her health first, not just start gabbing."

Doree huffed into the phone, but said nothing.

Spring cleared her throat. "Aunt Geneva has told me the full story of our mother's natural parents."

"Wow!" Doree exclaimed. "I can't believe you finally got her to tell."

Spring talked over Doree's voice. Tonight, Doree's flippant attitude irritated Spring like a fingernail scraping against a chalkboard. "Aunt Geneva decided we should know, in case mother ever needed or wanted to know. Aunt Geneva says she is the only living person who knows what happened."

"Does that mean that mother's natural father is deceased, too?" Hannah asked.

"I'm afraid so." Spring sighed again.

"When did he die?" Doree continued her interrogation. "Did he marry and have other children?"

Spring drew on her waning emotional reserves. *What are you getting at, Doree?* "He died when his ship was attacked in the Pacific in World War II."

Doree enquired, "Did anyone attend his funeral?"

Spring frowned. "I doubt anyone from Mother's hometown. He and our grandmother's friend, Connie Wilson, were engaged but not married. I think he might have gone down with his ship. Would they even have held a funeral service?"

"What was his name?" Doree pressed.

"Bill Smith." Spring couldn't keep the exhaustion out of her voice. *Stop it, Doree.*

"Bill Smith? That's an awfully common name," Doree commented.

"What of it?" Hannah countered.

"Well," Doree demanded, "so many Bill Smiths died in World War II, but maybe not our Bill Smith."

Chapter Thirteen

"What do you mean by that?" Spring asked, frustrated.

"I mean that it's not over until I find *the* Bill Smith who was or is our grandfather," Doree insisted. "Mistakes in reporting men who died in action have happened in every war."

"Do you really think that's possible?" Hannah asked, sounding uncertain.

"I'm not giving up until every avenue is exhausted. This is too crucial to Mom's health not to try," Doree said. "Spring, give me all the details you can remember about our grandfather."

Spring thought back over her aunt's words. "He was stationed at the Great Lakes Naval Base near Waukegan, Illinois. Connie and he met in Milwaukee, where she was working at a defense factory. His ship was attacked in the Pacific in 1945."

"That's all you've got?" Doree didn't sound

peeved, merely thorough. "I'm going to use the Internet for this search. You'd be surprised the kinds of government records that are open to the public and only a click away."

"Sounds like you know what you're doing," Spring conceded.

"If you get a chance—when it wouldn't upset her—you might ask Aunt Geneva if she knew what state or town he was from." Doree's concerned, businesslike tone surprised Spring. Maybe their baby sister was maturing.

"I will." Spring lay back on the bed, too exhausted to sit up. The cruise, Aunt's heart attack, everything!

"Spring?" Hannah's soft voice coaxed. "I know you're probably really tired, but my wedding plans are proceeding on schedule. When Mom comes to Florida, she's going to take your measurements for your maid-of-honor dress. I've chosen peach chiffon for the bridesmaids. It should look really good on you and Doree."

Hannah's June wedding. Spring had shoved it to the back of her mind, along with the fact that Mother would arrive in a few days. Now she tried to infuse her voice with some enthusiasm. "Peach will be lovely. I suppose you weren't able to dissuade Mother from sewing the bridesmaids' dresses?"

Hannah sighed with deep feeling. "It was a losing battle. She really wanted to do them, especially when I wouldn't let her sew my wedding gown."

"She's still making the veil, isn't she?" Doree put her oar in the conversation. "Her veils are always so elegant. And I hope you're not doing something *precious* for bridesmaid dresses. I don't want to have to bury the dress when I'm done.''

''You're insufferable,'' Hannah shot back. ''For a crack like that, I should add lace and ruffles to yours!''

''I have a headache,'' Spring announced, too worn down to take any more sisterly banter.

''We'll let you go,'' Hannah hurried to say. ''I'm sure you've been under a lot of stress. But I'm so glad you were there when Aunt Geneva needed you. Tell her I'm counting on her to recover and come to my wedding.''

''I'll tell her.'' Spring rolled toward the phone's cradle on the bedside table.

Doree piped up, ''When will you be back in Wisconsin?''

This stopped Spring in the act of hanging up. Should she tell them? She hadn't let anyone know of her intentions. ''I don't know—''

''But isn't your leave of absence up in a few more weeks?'' Hannah asked.

She decided to test out the reactions to her decision. ''I'm thinking of staying here—but don't say anything yet.''

''For good?'' Doree exclaimed. ''Does this have something to do with that guy who went on that cruise—?''

''On that note, good night, dear sisters. I love you.'' Spring hung up and closed her eyes. Hannah's wedding, Aunt Geneva's illness, Mother's coming, the Golden Sands April Garden Show, Marco's free clinic, Paloma's portrait—her mind was crowded with such a multitude of things to do, but all she wanted to think about, to savor, was the vivid memory of Marco's heart-stopping kisses.

Her phone rang. She picked it up, hoping Doree hadn't thought of any more questions. "Hello?"

"Spring?" Marco's rich voice asked.

She sat up, her pulse speeding up. "Marco?"

"I'm sorry to call you so late, but I thought you'd like to know—"

"Is something wrong with my aunt?" *No, Lord, please.*

"No, it's about the clinic. Pete called and said he and Greg filed the application for nonprofit status for the Gulfview Free Clinic today." The pride in his voice was palpable.

"That's wonderful."

"Pete says it will only take a week or two to be approved." His voice sounded hesitant, shy.

Why? Was it because of how their relationship was changing? "This is exciting." She forced enthusiasm into her voice, wishing they were speaking face-to-face. *Ah, yes.*

"It is." He paused. "When we have a chance, we need to celebrate."

"Yes," she managed to reply. Her heart was so full, she couldn't get any power from her diaphragm to speak more.

"I'll bid you *buenas noches,* then." His voice caressed her.

"Good night." Spring hung up the phone once more. Closing her eyes, she imagined Marco beside her, holding her. At the thought, sensations—warmth and chills—alternately cascaded through her. *Dear Lord, if Marco is the one for me, please tell me how to let him know I love him.*

Then another wonderful idea for the free clinic popped into her mind. Would it work?

At the sight of the airport minivan, Spring flung open her aunt's front door. "Mother!" She rushed out and threw her arms around her mother.

Ethel, in the navy-blue traveling suit Spring knew so well, stopped in the midst of giving the shuttle driver a tip and returned the hug. Then she turned back to the driver and thanked him. He looked at the tip, carried her bags to the door and left smiling.

Spring experienced crosscurrents of joy at seeing her mother. She worried, however, that she might accidentally let the facts of the search for her natural grandfather slip. Blocking these from her mind, she picked up the heaviest suitcase and ushered her mother inside. "I would have been happy to pick you up at the airport."

"No, I'm used to the shuttle and I only had to wait about fifteen minutes for it. How are you, dear? How's Aunty?"

"I'm fine!" Aunt Geneva called from her new recliner out in the Florida room at the back of her house. "Put the bags in your room, then come out here. Matilde has made fresh iced tea with lemon for us, and cucumber-and-dill sandwiches.''

Soon the four of them relaxed in the long, breezy room overlooking the garden. March rains had brought every leaf to a brilliant green and every bloom to a vivid pink, red or white. The shimmering turquoise Gulf framed the garden still life.

''This is the life.'' Mother sighed. ''I just left two feet of snow in Wisconsin.''

''I told you years ago that you and Garner should move to Florida,'' Aunty said in an I-told-you-so tone.

Mother smiled. ''We love Wisconsin. But I did need a break this year. You know I would have come down sooner, but Spring said I should wait until you were home. You're looking good. How are you feeling?''

''Like a new woman, or, at least, I will when I'm completely recovered.''

''Well, I hope that's in time for Hannah's wedding.''

''I wouldn't miss it! And we may have another wedding in the near future,'' Aunty said with a nod toward Spring.

Spring blushed. *I should have expected this!*

Mother glanced at Spring. ''Is it that young man you persuaded to go on the cruise?''

''*Sí!*'' Matilde answered for her. ''Marco Da Palma, the stepson of a dear friend of mine.''

Paloma in blue jeans and red T-shirt walked in.

"Matilde, I finished mopping the kitchen and all the bathrooms. What do you want me to do next?"

"Come and have a glass of iced tea," Aunty invited. "This is Spring's mother, Ethel Kirkland."

"Good morning, Mrs. Kirkland." Paloma smiled, then pointed to herself. "I'm Marco's little sister."

Mother returned the smile and greeted Paloma.

"Matilde, if Paloma has finished her chores, I'd like to get some more work done on her portrait," Spring said. "I've been so busy. But it's so close, I need to get it done."

"Of course!" Matilde got up. "Paloma, drink your tea, while I help Spring set up her easel. We only have a few Saturdays to go!"

Mother chuckled. "I see nothing has changed at your house, Aunty. Never a dull moment!"

On the Golden Sands veranda overlooking the green golf course, Spring sat back and sighed with contentment. She was about to initiate the plan she'd thought of to help Marco's clinic. At first, she'd dreaded being on the April Garden Show committee, but now she thought she detected the hand of God. The garden show would be the perfect vehicle for the plan that had unfolded in Spring's mind. She smiled at Aunt Geneva, Verna Rae and Eleanor, who ranged around the table.

"Ladies, I have a change in plans for this show I need to discuss with you three. I think this garden show is just what the doctor ordered...."

* * *

Spring watched Marco, tall and lithe, as he took a practice swing on the first tee. Another week had passed, bringing them closer to each other and to the April Garden Show. What would Marco think of what she'd set in motion?

Marco swung, connected with the ball and sent it flying over the fairway toward the green.

"Excellent!" Spring beamed at him.

He stood with his hands on his hips, watching the arc of his ball. "Not bad for a beginner."

She chuckled. "You're a natural and I hate you."

He grinned back at her.

She'd noticed Marco doing this more and more often. The dreadfully serious Dr. Da Palma was doing a vanishing act right before her eyes. "So golf isn't as bad as you thought?"

"It's addictive—and you knew that, didn't you," he said in a falsely accusatory tone.

She twirled the ends of an imaginary handlebar mustache. "Ha, ha, ha. It's all a part of my dark stratagem to make you have fun! I've got you in my clutches now, Doctor."

His sizzling smile to this silliness made her legs weak. She inhaled deeply, gathering her paper-thin resistance to this handsome man's potent charm.

His cell phone rang.

Spring tried not to look peeved, but they had yet to finish a golf lesson without at least one interruption.

Scowling, Marco pulled it out of his pocket and opened it. "Dr. Da Palma speaking."

Warm sunshine on her face, Spring closed her eyes and breathed in the salty Gulf air. The day couldn't be more perfect—if only Marco wouldn't be called away.

"Really!"

Spring hadn't ever heard Marco sound so excited. She opened her eyes wider and took a step closer.

"That's great! I can't believe it went through so easily. How can I thank you? Great. Sure. Thanks again." He snapped the phone shut.

She took another step closer.

"That was Pete—"

She gave a little hop of anticipation. "The nonprofit—"

"Status has been granted!" He threw his arms around her. "It's going to start—what I've dreamed of! And I owe it all to you!"

Breathless, she returned his embrace. "Not to me. I just got you started. God's blessing is written all over this. Pete and Greg just picked up the ball."

"I can't believe it!" He swung her up into his arms and kissed her.

Spring's breath caught in her throat. *Marco, I love you. When will I have the courage to tell you? And what will you say when I do?*

"Welcome! *Bienvenido a nuestro fiesta!* Welcome to our fiesta!" Anita greeted them in the driveway of her home.

Arriving at the fiesta to celebrate the clinic's achieving nonprofit status, Spring had dropped off her passengers and parked farther down the crowded block, then walked over. Now with her aunt, mother, Verna Rae and Eleanor at her side, she glanced around. The men had congregated in the front yard, sitting on the steps and grass. Santos waved cheerfully. She waved back as she scanned the male faces around Santos. No Marco.

After Spring introduced her mother, Verna Rae and Eleanor, Anita led them up the drive to the canopy in the backyard.

"*Por favor,* help yourselves to the food and drink. I'll find some chairs for you over in the shade."

"We're so thrilled for Marco!" Aunty announced. "You have a wonderful son! We think the world of him."

"*Gracias.*" Anita blushed. "The members of Golden Sands all did so much for Marco. I can't thank you enough for helping my son with his education."

"It was our pleasure," Eleanor said. "We love to see worthy students achieve their ambitions."

Verna Rae nodded vigorously. "It's the American dream, and we like to do our part to see it keeps happening."

The backyard overflowed with women and children. Spring waved hello to Paloma, who was surrounded by her young friends. *Tía* Rosita and Lupe from Mamacita's were pushing two little girls on the swing set. They waved to Spring. The happy scene reminded her of a church picnic. She glanced around discreetly for Marco.

"Hello." He appeared at her elbow. "I'm so glad all of you could come."

All the ladies with Spring fluttered around Marco, congratulating him. Spring couldn't control her face, which insisted on breaking into a ridiculously wide smile. Mother stood apart until the rush died down.

"Marco, I'd like you to meet my mother," Spring said. Mother held out her hand, and Marco shook it. Spring tried to look nonchalant, but she could tell by the assessing look her mother gave Marco that Aunty had divulged even more about Spring's interest in him. Fortunately, her mother wasn't the type to make mortifying comments.

"Hey! Spring!" Pete, wearing a University of Florida T-shirt and cutoffs, bounded over.

Spring smiled at him but mentally crossed her fingers. What would unpredictable Pete say?

"Brought plenty of chaperones, I see!" Pete announced to the world at large. "Good idea! Marco's quite the Don Juan!"

She could always count on Pete to be excruciatingly tactless. "Does anyone have a gag I could borrow?" she said wryly.

"Hey! I just call 'em like I see 'em," Pete announced.

She glanced at Marco to see his reaction. He didn't look like he'd even noticed Pete's teasing. His warm regard, centered on her, brought a blush that worked an intense path throughout her body.

She imagined Marco's reaction to the surprise she

was busy working on. He'd be so happy. They'd celebrate with another fiesta!

Spring trailed the elderly real estate agent and Marco inside the empty downtown church, just a stone's throw away from Mamacita's and the Hacienda Bakery. It must have been empty well over a year. Broken windows had been boarded up and cobwebs fluttered from the high ceiling in the breeze from the open front doors. In the neglected sanctuary, the stained-glass window behind the pulpit still translated sunshine into brilliant blue, gold and red beams of light, cast over the dusty interior.

"Well, you've seen it all, then," the rotund real estate agent said. "Any other questions?"

"I don't think so." Marco's eye roved over the large room. "I'll stop at the bank and get the financing and paperwork started."

"Okay. I'll be going, then. Are you and the lady staying?"

Marco looked to Spring. "We'll look around just a bit longer."

"Then, be sure to lock up."

Marco and the man shook hands. When the realtor had departed, Marco ambled over to Spring and sat down beside her on an old wooden pew. Seeking connection with her, he slid his arm around her shoulder. For many minutes, they sat in silence. Did Spring feel the way he did about being here?

"It's very satisfying, isn't it," she said, answering his unspoken question.

"It's a start," he admitted. He stroked Spring's arm with the hand that secured her to him. "I'm glad you agreed to come with me."

She looked up at him. "I was so happy you asked me to join you! This location is perfect. A good-size parking lot. The bus stop right on the corner. And there's room for expansion in the open area at the rear."

He drew in a deep breath. So much had happened in the past few months—ever since Spring had come back into his life. "I think I'll send the garden show committee ladies roses."

"Roses?" She gave him an arch look. Had someone let her surprise slip out ahead of time? "Why?"

"Because if they hadn't guilted me onto the committee, you wouldn't have come back into my life."

Spring lost her breath for a moment, then she inhaled deeply. "I feel the same way."

"You do?" Marco looked as if he couldn't believe it.

"Yes." She nodded, then decided to let actions speak louder than words. She kissed him.

He turned her in his embrace and gathered her closer. He kissed her.

She closed her eyes, concentrating all of her senses on the touch of his lips on hers and the delicious rush of pleasure his caress brought her. "Marco," she whispered against his mouth, "I love you."

Her own words shocked her. But she couldn't mistake Marco's actions. He wasn't a man to kiss a woman whom he didn't—

"I've loved you since the first time I saw you in Professor Warnock's freshman biology class," he murmured.

Her breath caught in her throat again.

He kissed her.

"Why didn't you let me know?" she asked, dazed at hearing his declaration of love.

He shrugged. "How could I? You were so beautiful, so aloof, so blond! And I had no time or money for dating."

She nestled her face in the curve of his neck. "We were both too young, I guess. That was my very first college class. I was so nervous that day, I felt sick."

He chuckled against her ear, a lovely sensation to her. "Every guy in the room had a hard time keeping his eyes on the prof. They were all sneaking peeks at you."

She shook her head. "I didn't—don't—like it when men do that."

He nodded. "It made you shy, didn't it?"

She looked up at him. "You understand that?"

"Yes, you never liked men hanging all over you, and then that night..." He let his voice fade.

She appreciated his tact. He was bringing up one of the worst nights of her life. She snuggled closer to him. "I've never forgotten how you rescued me that night."

"And I regret I didn't get to break that guy's nose. That's what I wanted to do! I still think you should have reported him to the university. He was a pig." Marco's handsome face darkened with anger.

His strong reaction after all these years—was it an indication of how he felt about her?

That dreadful night, she'd gone out with a blind date. It had started as a double date, but the other couple had wanted to neck. Uncomfortable with this turn of events, Spring had asked her date to walk her back to her dorm. On the way, he pulled her off the lighted path into the bushes. He'd made it clear he wanted more than necking. Frightened, she'd run away from him—straight into Marco, who'd been walking home from the library. Marco had sent her "date" on his way and walked her back to her dorm himself.

"I'd have liked to give him a black eye along with the broken nose, but I didn't think you wanted to make a big deal out of it."

"You did just what you should have." She sighed. "That all seems a million years ago."

"And I feel like a different man since you came into my life again. And the cruise—it opened my eyes to how much I was still carrying the past around with me."

"What do you mean?"

"You were right. I was still thinking of myself as different from everyone because of being an Hispanic immigrant and having to pay for school by working and…charity."

"Scholarships," she corrected him. "You shouldn't have let that bother you. A lot of students—"

He pressed his finger to her lips, then kissed her

right, then her left, eyebrow. "I'm seeing things clearly now. Yes, I faced discrimination when I was younger. But I've been holding onto it in a way that...was keeping me from life...from you."

She lost her breath again. She inhaled, trying to reel in her rampant reactions. "Let's leave the past *in the past.*"

"I plan to...focus on the future." He ran his fingers into her hair, lifting it and watching it fall. "I achieved my goal to become a doctor. Now my objective to provide free medical services can begin. It will take years, but I don't mind."

She nearly voiced her good news for him then, but squelched it. The work wasn't finished yet. She'd wait until the right time, then surprise him. She traced the bow of his sculpted lips.

In response, he outlined the line of her ivory cheek with his forefinger. "When do you have to go back to Wisconsin?"

She thrilled at his touch. "I don't. I've resigned my position. I'm staying in Florida."

His eyes widened with surprise. "You are? You want to move here? I hadn't...I'd hoped...."

"Aunty needs me, and I just couldn't bear to go back—"

He cut off her words with another kiss.

She didn't mind at all. The future, their future looked so bright. And the best was yet to come. The garden show was just around the corner. She still had a lot of work to do before then, but she'd accomplished her goal for Marco, the man she loved and who loved her.

She whispered, "You'll be coming to the garden show, won't you?"

"Do you want me to?" Grinning, he nudged her nose with his.

"Yes, I think it would mean a lot to Verna Rae, Eleanor and Aunty." *And me. And you.*

"I'll be there, then."

Chapter Fourteen

The phone in Aunty's front hall jingled. "I'll get it," Spring called out, and picked up the beige receiver. "Hello."

"Spring! You'll never guess!" Doree shouted, "I found him! I found our grandfather! I just talked to him on the phone!"

Spring's mouth opened but no words came out.

"Did you hear me?"

"You talked to our grandfather?" Spring swallowed with difficulty. "He's alive?"

"Alive and kicking!" Doree crowed. "He retired to Long Beach, California."

"How did you find him, Doree?" Spring's mind raced. "I can hardly believe what you're saying."

"Believe it! I just started by finding out all the Bill or William Smith's who'd served in the Navy in World War II, trained at Great Lakes and were reported dead or wounded in the Pacific in 1945. You'd be amazed at the information I found.''

Spring tried to put the brakes on Doree's runaway enthusiasm. "How do you know he's Mother's biological father?"

"Because I asked him."

"You asked him!" *No, Doree, no!* "We all agreed not to contact Mother's natural family unless we had to—"

"I didn't ask him about Mother. But after all the hours of research, I had to call him. I was just going to act like I was doing research on World War II veterans who'd been mistakenly reported lost in action, but he was so nice. I ended up asking him if he'd known a woman named Connie Wilson."

"Doree, you didn't!" They should have known not to leave an issue so delicate up to Doree. "How could you?"

"Well, I could and I did. And he said yes he'd been engaged to a Connie Wilson in Milwaukee in 1945, but that she'd died while he was away at sea. He even said that after he'd recovered from being wounded, he went to her hometown. But her parents wouldn't speak to him, except to tell him Connie was dead and that they didn't want to have anything to do with him."

"He did?" The cruelty of her great-grandparents withholding the truth about their daughter and her child from the man she loved made her chest tighten as though they'd pierced her own heart. "Why didn't they tell him the truth? That he had a daughter?"

"I don't know. But he said it took him nearly ten years to get over losing her. He didn't marry again until 1956. And get this, sis, he's got three grown children."

"Mother has half brothers and sisters!" This was more than she'd ever expected!

"Yes." Doree sounded smug. "Three other possible donors, if Mom should need them."

"Praise God. This is almost too much to take in all at once."

"That's why I didn't tell him that I was his natural granddaughter. I didn't want to give him a heart attack."

A movement in Spring's peripheral vision made her pause. *Oh, no!* "Mother?"

Looking dazed, Mother walked out from the doorway to the living room. "What have you girls done?"

Spring tightened her grip on the receiver. "Doree, Mother's here in the hallway."

"Oh, no!" Doree moaned into Spring's ear.

Taking a deep breath, Spring turned to face her mother. "Doree, Hannah and I have been trying to locate your natural parents—"

"You know I told you I didn't want you to do that!" Mother's voice quavered.

Spring had never seen her mother this pale, or shaking the way she was. "Mother, here, sit down." Spring pulled out the chair from the phone table.

Mother sat down, but in spite of her wan face her expression turned stormy. "Why did you go against—"

"We had to. If one of us had matched as a bone marrow donor, we wouldn't have pursued this."

"But—"

"But what if your remission ended. We couldn't take the chance."

Looking somber, Aunt Geneva walked out of another doorway. "I overheard you, too. I think we all ought to sit down and talk this over calmly. Tell Doree we'll call her back in a bit."

Spring obeyed her aunt, grateful for backup.

Frighteningly white now, Mother looked up. "You knew about this, Aunty?"

"Yes, and it's all for the best—if Bill did indeed survive. Don't you realize that he loved your mother and would have wanted you?"

Mother began to weep.

Aunty looked to Spring. "Let's all go out in the Florida room. It's time for all the old secrets and pain to come out into the light of truth."

An hour and a full box of blue tissues later, the tragic love story of her natural parents had been revealed to Mother.

Holding the receiver again with Doree on the line, Spring watched her mother wipe her eyes.

"I wish this…had been explained…to me years ago," Mother said haltingly. "I always thought that my natural parents didn't want me." She inhaled deeply, her tears drying. "That's why I was so adamant about not trying to locate them. I didn't want to be rejected twice."

"Oh, Ethel," Aunt Geneva lamented, "if I or your mother Gloria had known, we would have told you. Your natural parents loved one another and would have been married—if only Connie's parents had kept their noses out of things."

"Let me talk to Doree again." Mother reached out her hand for the phone. "Doree, call Mr. Smith back, tell him about what happened to…my mother, his sweetheart, and ask him if he'd like to meet me. If he truly loved my mother, I'll take the chance."

"Wow, Mom. I will." Doree hung up.

"Time will tell." Aunty sighed. "Now I'm ready for some lunch. I feel like I've just chopped a pile of wood. And I've never lifted an ax in my life!"

Though still teary, Mom chuckled at this.

Spring felt her spirits lift again. Only the tiniest doubt remained that Grandfather Smith would refuse to talk to Mother. *Oh, Lord, after years of misunderstanding and pain, please let this be a time of happy reunion!*

The April Garden Show judging had nearly ended. The airy Golden Sands Country Club, open to the public for the day, teemed and hummed with well-dressed residents and tourists in shorts and T-shirts, examining the colorful prize plants. In one area, an extensive variety of blooming orchids had been judged, while in another, tea roses of every shade were displayed. The main corridor was devoted to an educational display of Bird of Paradise. Area nurseries and greenhouses had set up sample garden displays on the lawn. The show had broken all past attendance records.

In the midst of stellar success, Spring's only problem was that Marco still hadn't shown up. And it was almost time!

"What's keeping him?" Aunt Geneva in a purple dress with gold buttons fretted for the tenth time.

"I don't know."

Eleanor appeared at Spring's elbow, her floral-print chiffon skirt swishing about her. "That Marco, where is he?"

"I don't know." Spring couldn't hold back the nerves eating at her stomach. "He promised me faithfully that he'd be here."

"Well," Verna Rae crowded closer to Eleanor, "if he isn't here, we'll just have to go on without him."

Spring worried her lower lip. *No, Marco, not another emergency call from the hospital.* "That's the head judge signaling to me. They're ready to hand out the prize ribbons."

"No stopping now," Aunty said in bracing tones. "We'll just have to proceed—Marco or no Marco."

Spring nodded, her optimism drooping by the second. She and the other three garden show committee members walked to the front of the large ballroom, which was filling with attendees taking their seats to see the prizes bestowed on winners and take part in the second part of the gala.

One last time, Spring turned back to the entrance. Marco strode in and paused, looking around. She stood on tiptoe and waved at him. *He's here! He won't miss it!*

She wondered if the happiness she concealed would burst out of bounds before the time came to reveal the joyful news for Marco. It was only minutes now!

Marco wended his way through the crowd toward her. Dressed in a black suit with a white shirt and silver tie, he was more devastatingly striking than she'd ever thought him before. His mere glance turned her into sweet, melted joy. *Marco, my love.*

Spring saw the transformation in him, which had come in the past few weeks. Smiling, he stopped to greet Golden Sands members and other friends, shaking hands and nodding toward her, the picture of easy but dignified charm. *My cup runneth over, Lord. Aunty's health is improving. I'm staying in Florida, and Marco and I have a future, a wonderful future ahead of us. Thank You, Lord. It's almost too many blessings to believe. I accept them with a grateful heart.*

Marco reached her and put his arm around her shoulder as though they'd been a couple for a thousand years. A glow like tropical sunshine coursed through her.

Happiness and thankfulness clogged Spring's throat. *This wonderful man loves me!* She tried to tell him everything with her smile. *Marco, I love you.*

She and Marco sank down side by side in the front row. He knit his long, tanned fingers with hers. This simple act made her heart hum with a silent ecstatic melody. Aunt Geneva went to the podium, and for the next fifteen minutes, prizes in various categories were awarded to beaming winners. When this had been wrapped up, Aunty signaled to Spring.

Shaking inside but exultant, Spring stood up and made her way to the podium. Love expanding within her, she let herself send a special glance to Marco. His eyebrows were lifted in question. She sent him a tremulous smile, then cleared her throat.

"As you know, the Golden Sands April Garden Show is in its thirty-fifth year. This year the Golden Sands board approved an addition to the program which we hope will become a part of this yearly event."

Spring drew in a deep breath. "As you probably noticed, a silent auction has been in progress all during today's show. Many generous Golden Sands members, local merchants and contestants have donated goods, services and prize-worthy plants to be auctioned off to benefit a new community project initiated by Dr. Marco Da Palma—the Gulfview Free Clinic."

Looking at Marco, she noted that he'd frozen in his chair. Well, she'd wanted to surprise him and she certainly had!

"While the grand total of the money generated by today's silent auction is being calculated, I'd like to thank several community leaders who instantly took to this idea and have already made sizable pledges. Would those people please come forward now?"

She stole a peek at Marco's face. She couldn't decipher his expression. What was he thinking?

She continued. ''First, I'd like to mention that Peter Rasmussen and Gregory Fortney have donated the money for the down payment for the clinic's site, the former Faith Community Church on Main Street. They couldn't be here today, but send their best. Now—'' she motioned toward a fashionable couple in their forties who stepped up to meet her ''—this couple is Mr. and Mrs. Grady Jones. They have volunteered to pay the first year's monthly mortgage for the clinic.''

Applause broke out. The Joneses said a few words, then stepped back. Next, Spring introduced the three different contracting firms who had offered to update the clinic's plumbing, electrical and handicapped accessibility, gratis. Applause greeted each announced donation.

Spring glanced at Marco. His face was devoid of any reaction. *What's wrong, Marco?*

A Golden Sands board member approached the podium and handed her a sheet of yellow paper. Seeing the total, she beamed. ''Today's silent auction has netted the Gulfview Free Clinic $9,352.00 in cash.''

The audience exploded into reverberating applause. A few men stomped their feet and whistled. Spring felt tears fill her eyes. *Thank you, Lord. You have moved people to such generosity, it takes my breath away.*

Marco looked like he'd stopped breathing, too. Should she have warned him or given him a hint?

Sitting beside Marco's mother, stepfather and sister, Matilde and *Tía* Rosita rose. They both marched forward like women with a mission. Spring stepped back and let them have the microphone.

"I'm Matilde Ramirez and this is *Tía* Rosita. We don't have a lot of money, but we are going to make sure—with help from other women in the downtown community—that this will be the cleanest clinic in Florida!"

More applause.

But Marco sat, blank-faced and immobile.

Spring tried to think what to say, to do. What was Marco thinking?

In the back of the ballroom, a man stood up. Spring thought she recognized him and motioned toward him to speak. He raised his strong voice. "I'm Dr. Edward Clary. I'm the head of staff at Gulfview General and I work with Dr. Da Palma. I hadn't heard of these plans, but I'm certain that many of the doctors and nurses of Gulfview will be willing to donate time at the clinic—"

The room exploded with excitement. Many people stood to applaud. Soon the whole roomful was on its feet. The chant of "Speech, speech" began.

Spring eyed Marco. Would he come to the podium? Mother, who sat beside him, pushed him to his feet. He walked to the front as though his joints had stiffened. Abashed and uncertain, Spring stepped aside so he could speak into the microphone.

Marco looked out over the sea of happy faces and felt like slamming his fist into the podium. He took a steadying breath, spooling in his rage. *I have to get through this.*

"Ladies and gentlemen," he began, feeling his way carefully toward the proper words, not the ones he stuffed down inside, unsaid. "I had no idea—" *that's for sure* "—that today's garden show...would hold so many surprises. I'm stunned." *That's the truth.* "But Spring Kirkland appears to be full of surprises." *Shocks is more like it.* There was laughter.

"This clinic...which will provide free medical care for those who have insufficient insurance, no insurance or don't qualify for any government assistance, is vitally necessary in our community." Speaking about the clinic steadied him. He unclenched his right fist.

"To those of you who have donated items for auction, thank you. To those who have pledged time and money, I'm deeply indebted to you...." This grated his already raw nerves. *But I never wanted to be.*

Stifling his anger, he motioned for the new applause to quiet. "Thank you all, especially Spring Kirkland, whom I'm sure is responsible for all this." The unkindest cut of all. *How could you, Spring? How could you?*

The next afternoon, Spring stood, fretting in the parking lot of the Golden Sands golf course. The blue sky overhead, the tantalizing warm breeze, the gorgeous day counted for nothing. She consulted her watch again. Marco was twenty-two minutes late for their golf date. *He isn't coming.* The words echoed like a death knell inside her.

Something had gone dreadfully, dreadfully wrong yesterday afternoon at the garden show. Somehow everything fresh and sparkling between Marco and her had disappeared in a flash. After the announcements of all the support for the free clinic, she'd stood beside him, accepting congratulations. But it had been like standing beside a glacier. *What is it, Lord? What did I do to anger him?*

With a feeling of fatalism, she flipped open her cell phone and dialed his apartment. No answer. She punched in his office number. No answer. She shrank from calling the hospital. As a last resort before giving up, she dialed his mother's number. ''Hello, Anita, this is Spring. I'm trying to locate Marco. We had a golf date today.''

''Oh, Spring, he just called me about something. He's at the church.''

Did she detect worry in Anita's voice? ''The church for the free clinic?''

''*Sí.* Do you have his cell phone number?'' Anita asked.

Spring said yes, thanked her and hung up. She stared out across the green to the rippling blue Gulf beyond. *Lord, I feel like running home, crying my eyes out and hiding in my room for the next month. But that's the old Spring. I've come too far to go back. I won't lose the man I love a second time. But You're going to have to go with me and give me the words to say—because I haven't got a clue what's wrong!*

Spring parked her aunt's car in the littered parking lot on the west side of the white stucco church, then walked to its side entrance. Her heart pounded in her ears, louder with each step. What would she say? What would Marco say? Closing her eyes, she said one more prayer for guidance, then she opened the door and walked in. Immediately, she heard the *swish* of a broom and knew she'd probably find Marco at the handle end of it.

With flagging steps, she entered the sanctuary. Head down, Marco was sweeping the refuse in front of the pulpit into a neat pile. His posture telegraphed his despondent mood to her. *What is it, Marco?*

"Hello," she called, and paused by the last row of wooden pews. She remembered how they'd sat side by side here, sharing how much in love they were, such a short time ago.

Marco looked up. No smile welcomed her.

"We had a golf date." Her voice quavered in the empty, high-ceilinged room.

"Golf?" He sounded as if he didn't recognize the word.

"You know, the game where you hit the little ball into a cup?" She attempted a smile but it faded under his sober attention.

"I'm sorry. I guess I forgot."

His tone chilled her. Marco never forgot. A tremor of naked fear arced through her.

He made a sound of disgust, then rested both wrists

atop the broom handle. "I didn't forget. I just didn't feel like golf today. I meant to call you. I just didn't…get to the phone."

She fought to remain calm. "Marco, I—"

"I'm sorry I made you track me down." He cut her off in a flat voice.

The sharp look he gave her made her freeze inside. Who was this cold-eyed stranger? It couldn't be her Marco.

"I—I see," she stuttered, tears only a breath away. "Well, I'll let you get back to work." Her brightly spoken words tripped over her tongue. "We can set up another date."

He nodded as if she'd just said, "Let's discuss that at the next funeral."

Before tears could overtake her, she turned and ran outside. She sprinted to her car.

Inside, a gale of weeping broke over her. Her head bowed, she sobbed into her hands. Mental photographs of moments spent with Marco flashed in a parade in her mind—Marco frowning over a golf shot, Marco doing the limbo, Marco in the moonlight…

Finally the tempest passed, leaving her weak and shaky. She prayed for calm and waited for it. Finally, still distraught, she started her car. She had to get home, home to Mother.

She found her mother in her aunt's garden. Without a word, but with tears flowing, she walked into her mother's arms. *This is what it feels like to have a broken heart. Oh, God, it hurts so bad. What has happened?*

Mother held her close and murmured soft words to her, just as she had when Spring was a child. Slowly, Spring's tears ebbed.

"It's Marco, isn't it," Mother murmured beside Spring's ear.

Spring nodded, too exhausted emotionally to speak.

"I could see how he changed at the garden show. You don't have a clue why, do you?"

Shaking her head no, Spring caught her breath. "I thought he loved me."

"He does, dear. But without meaning to, yesterday you triggered something inside him. I don't know him so I don't have a clue what it might be."

"I didn't just imagine it?" Spring straightened and accepted the tissue her mother handed her.

"No, dear, I saw it, too."

"What do I do?" A stray sob shook Spring, then made her hiccup.

"Have you asked the Lord for his help?"

"Yes." *What else could I do?*

"Then, you've done all you can do. Just keep praying to God and loving Marco. Marco is an honest man, a man of integrity. When he sorts everything out, he'll come to his senses and tell you what's happened."

Spring closed her eyes, praying her mother was right, and that it wouldn't take another decade for Marco to come back to her.

* * *

Letting an hour pass after Spring's call, Anita decided she must take action. Fortunately, Paloma was at a friend's house. Santos had been called away by someone's plumbing emergency. She had the house to herself—the perfect time. She called Marco's cell phone number.

Marco answered.

She noted his dull voice. *No es un hombre feliz.* Not a happy man.

She tested her guess. "Is Spring still there?"

"No, she just stopped for a moment. I forgot our golf date."

Anita wasn't pleased to be proved right.

"Marco, I need you here pronto. It's an emergency."

"Mama—"

She hung up on him. And sat back to wait.

In exactly twenty-one minutes, Marco's car surged up her driveway. She rose, poured a fresh cup of black coffee for each of them.

He bounded in the kitchen door. "What's wrong?"

She turned to face him. *"You're wrong."* She handed him the coffee mug. "Sit down. It's time we had a talk."

He stared at her. "What?"

"Sit down, *por favor,*" she ordered.

Marco slid into the chair across from her at the scarred kitchen table that Santos had been nagging her to replace.

"Will you please tell me—"

"You hurt that sweet girl. She loves you, and you sent her away, didn't you."

"I don't know—"

"She loves you." She traced one of the grooves in the wooden tabletop. "Do you have any idea how rare true, real love is in this world?"

He stared at her. "Are you going to tell me what this is all about?"

"*Sí.* I watched the change in you at the garden show. Spring spent hours, days, weeks getting all the funds together so that you could have your clinic up and started by the end of this year, not ten years from now. And that's what's killing you, isn't it."

Her son glared at her.

She lifted her chin to him. "You wanted to work for years and do it *all by yourself,* didn't you?"

Her question had shocked him. She saw it on his face. "We should have had this talk years ago."

"What do you mean by that?"

Anita bit her lower lip. "It's always been difficult for us to speak of your father's death."

"Then, don't." He looked away, as he always did.

"We must. The time has come for you to let go of the past."

"I'm not holding onto the past."

She ignored his denial. "When your father died, something deep inside you altered. You had been a normal, happy child before that night. From that day, you became quiet and so focused on becoming a doctor."

"What is wrong with that? I had to be focused or…"

Seeking warmth, she placed both hands around the hot mug. "I know. You would never have reached your goals unless you had drawn out the best that was in you. We were poor. I knew you'd have to fight for your place in the world, so I said nothing. I never tried to speak to you about this. But after you completed your training and bought your practice, I hoped that you would begin to take time to have a life. I have worried and worried over you the past two years."

He looked startled. "You never said a word."

"Would words have helped? I hoped some young woman would snare your heart. I even stooped to bringing some to your attention, something I'd vowed never to do."

He made a sound of disgust and wouldn't meet her gaze.

"Then this year, Spring came into your life. I knew right away that she was special and that you had feelings for her. You changed before my eyes. I thank God for her. Now you are not going to let your pride and pain destroy your life and hers. I refuse to let this happen."

"Destroy my life? You're not making sense."

"*You* are not making sense. Did you want a free clinic in that church or didn't you?" She challenged him with her eyes.

Marco fumed in silence. *This is none of your business.*

"Answer me."

"Yes, I wanted the free clinic—"

"But you wanted to do it all on your own. *Qué tonto!* What a silly man. How many years would it have taken you to raise the funds for it?"

"Not that long." He evaded his mother's penetrating eyes.

"Years! It would have taken years on your own. Should the sick people have to wait that long? To serve your pride!"

Stung, he snapped, "That's not true."

"That is how it looks to me. Tell me how it looks to you." She stared at him.

Anger roiled in the pit of his stomach. Words, phrases spun in his mind. His mother's accusation echoed in his heart. Pride? Was it really pride? Or something else?

"Why are you so angry at me now, at Spring?" she demanded. "You are angry because she stepped into your dream and made it come true, when you were too proud to ask. You wanted to spend years struggling to do this alone. You would deny others the joy of helping you accomplish a fine goal. Pride is the only answer I can think of. She hurt your pride because she did it quicker and easier than you could have alone. Tell me I'm wrong and make me believe it."

He wanted to tell her she was wrong, but he had no words. He couldn't lie. He had been so angry, he hadn't been able to think straight—not yet. Was his mother right?

"And I hate to say this to you, *mi hijo,* but it is the worst kind of pride. Putting your own accomplishment ahead of the well-being of others is wrong."

He couldn't reply. How could he make her understand? *It isn't just pride. The clinic was my task, my penance....*

"You're not God. He can do things in his way and use whom He chooses. Now, confess your pride to God, then get down on your knees and thank Him for bringing you a wonderful woman like Spring who loves you with her whole heart. She is a blessing from heaven." His mother got up and walked from the room.

His mother's words had gouged him like a sharp chisel. Each word had hit its target—his pride. Should *Tía* Rosita and others continue to go without health care because of him? Marco sat stunned by his mother's truth.

But something else tugged at him. He thought back over that painful night when his father died. For so many years he'd blocked the wrenching memories. His mother had said that he'd changed from that night, and she'd been right. What had he felt during the accident?

All the raw emotions, details—he let them rip through him. The odor of gasoline, the smell of burnt rubber, a blaring faraway siren, his own tears choking him. His father, gasping for breath, had held Marco's small trembling hand in his large rough palm and had left him. Horror had twisted inside him, squeezing him, leaving him breathless, crushed. Padre, *don't leave me.*

What had he felt that night? Had it been pride? No, he'd felt useless, filled with regret, remorse, guilt.

Marco rubbed his forehead and bowed his head. He didn't pray often away from church—but was this a mistake, too? Was it another token of his self-sufficient pride?

"I'm sorry, God. I forgot that I am just dust. I see my pride and I'm ashamed. Please forgive me. But now I know guilt played a part in this also."

Still aching from his foray into the past, he remained with his head bowed for a long time as he pondered the years since his father's death. He'd driven himself from accomplishment to accomplishment. Guilt had been the whip that spurred him on. But in the achieving of goals, he'd depended on himself alone and no one else.

In his guilt, he'd let no one in. No man is an island, but he'd been a proud aloof island, and pride comes before a fall. Yesterday he'd fallen—he'd turned away from Spring, the beautiful and loving woman he'd fallen for at first sight. *How can I ever make it up to her? Will she give me a second chance?*

Chapter Fifteen

Marco drove directly to Spring. He bounded to her aunt's door and knocked.

Matilde opened the door. Glaring, she folded her hands across her ample waist. "You."

Her accusatory tone matched his self-recriminations. He drew in a deep breath. "I need to talk to Spring."

"You need to get down on your knees and kiss her hand."

"I intend to."

Matilde stepped back. "Then, you can come in. Spring! Marco is here for you."

A few moments later, Spring hung back at the other end of the hall. Her red-rimmed eyes belied her calm face. He noted her aunt standing behind her.

"Spring, will you go for a walk on the beach with me?"

She hesitated.

"You can go," Matilde said. "He's gonna apologize."

"He'd better apologize," Aunt Geneva added.

Marco held out his hand, and Spring came to him, but with downcast eyes. Her crestfallen look sliced him like a scalpel. Trying to think of the right words, he led her out the door. They followed the path through the gate down to the beach. The sun had passed its zenith. The beach was deserted except for an old woman and a little girl with copper curls who danced barefoot in the shallow surf. Sea foam puffed on the sand and diminutive crabs sidled away from their footsteps.

"Spring, I..." His voice faltered. "I apologize for acting like a jerk, an ungrateful jerk."

"Why?" Her voice was muffled against the sound of the waves. "What were you so angry about at the garden show? You wanted the clinic. Now you have it."

Marco plunged on. "But don't you see, I wanted it *my way*. I wanted to do it all by myself. I would have bumbled around for years trying to fund the clinic. I wouldn't have had a life, just a mission, a selfish one—even though it might have looked selfless. I didn't want your help. I didn't even want God's."

"Why?"

He struggled with himself, then decided to let go, tell her the unvarnished truth. "Do you remember when I told you about my father's death?"

She nodded but still wouldn't meet his eyes.

He halted and reached for her. After lifting her chin, he took her slender shoulders in both his hands. He'd look her in the eye—even though it pained him to speak of this. "I told you that watching my father die made me want to be a doctor. But more than that happened that night. Somehow I've felt responsible for my father's death...because I couldn't save him. I know it's not realistic—"

"But feelings are like that." Spring spoke in a shy voice as though they'd never spoken of love.

Like we're strangers, no! Don't shut me out, Spring! "I drove myself to be a doctor. Then, when I'd achieved that goal, I found another goal to sacrifice myself to."

"You mean, the clinic?"

"*Sí.* If I wasn't flogging myself toward another altruistic goal, I was failing."

"Just as you'd failed your father?"

She understands! He swallowed with difficulty. "*Sí.*"

"What does that mean to us? Is there an 'us'?" she asked, now looking into his eyes.

"I certainly hope so. Can you forgive me? I was wrong—"

She stopped his words with a kiss.

He wrapped his arms around her and put everything he had into his response.

A child's excited voice shrilled in the quiet. "Gramma, look! They're kissing. That man and lady are *kissing!*" The little girl giggled.

Spring started to giggle against his lips.

He felt her whole body shake with mirth. Pulling away an inch, he shouted, "Yes, I'm kissing her! And I'm proposing!" He slipped down onto one knee in the wet sand and claimed her hand. "Spring Kirkland, will you be my wife—even if I am a stubborn and proud man?"

She threw her head back and laughed out loud.

"Yes, Marco, I'll be your wife!" she shouted, then tugged him to stand up.

The little girl shrieked with glee, "Gramma, he was on his knee and now she's laughing!"

He swept Spring to him and kissed her with abandon. The sun golden on his back, the splash and ebb of the waves, the little girl's laughter, Spring's warm, soft form and his own joy—all flowing upward through him like a geyser. He'd never forget this moment for the rest of his life. *I'll never be alone again, Lord! I thank You—a thousand times, gracias!*

"Hi, Spring, this is—"

"Doree," Spring cut in.

"How's Mom?"

"Fine." Spring was afraid to ask the question uppermost in her mind. Her heart started beating faster.

"I'm here, too." Hannah's voice came over the line.

Spring had been planning to call Hannah herself, but it was ominous to have her sisters set up a conference call without warning her. "What's happened? Tell me."

"We have wonderful news!" Doree squealed.

"Our grandfather and his three children are going to come to Hannah's wedding!"

"What?"

Hannah took over. "Doree called and explained who she was and everything that had happened to Connie Wilson."

Doree burst in with her news. "He said that after he was wounded, he was laid up for a long time. He said he wanted to be well and able to support Connie before he returned to her. When he visited her parents, they told him she'd died, but he never knew anything about Connie having a baby—"

Hannah interrupted, "He said if he'd known, he would have taken Mother and raised her himself!"

Gladness for the present and sorrow over the past made it hard for Spring to speak, but she forced the words out. "Wait. Mother is the one who needs to hear this." She called for Mother and handed her the phone. "Doree has news for you."

Paloma's *quinceañería,* her fifteenth birthday party, was in full swing. A band played salsa music on a platform in the backyard. Children in their Sunday best danced around the adults on the driveway. A long table with nachos, enchiladas, frijoles, along with black beans, rice and plantains had been set up. On the grill, fragrant hamburgers, hot dogs and lime-basted chicken sizzled. Ladies in lawn chairs bordered the backyard fence. Out on the front porch and steps, the men congregated, laughing and joking.

At a picnic table, Marco sat at Spring's side holding her hand, which was adorned by a tasteful diamond engagement ring.

His mother and Spring's were admiring for the thousandth time the pastel portrait of Paloma that Spring had finished just a day before the party.

"I didn't know that Spring was an artist," his mother said, "but she did a fine job with our Paloma."

"She has a good eye," Mother admitted with modesty.

"I will treasure this always." His mother wiped her eyes.

"This is a thrilling time for both of you!" Aunt Geneva said. "A double June wedding for Hannah and Guthrie—"

"And for Spring and Marco!" his mother added with a smile.

"And I'm going to meet my father and my three half brothers and sister." Ethel dabbed her eyes, too. "You and Santos must stay with us, along with Aunty. We have plenty of room!"

"We would be honored." His mother's smile became mischievous. "Anyway, who knows? Next year we might be *abuelas*—grandmothers!"

Epilogue

The biggest predicament at Hannah's and Spring's double June wedding had brought a lot of different opinions—until a solution finally dawned on everyone.

Having a double wedding had sounded so efficient. After waiting for over a decade, Spring and Marco couldn't bear to spend a whole year making their own wedding plans. Hannah and Guthrie had made all their wedding plans and had been thrilled to share the day with Spring and Marco.

Now Hannah and Spring, dressed in their white gowns and the veils their mother had made them, waited in the Petite church vestibule. Spring couldn't hold back a few tears of joy.

"Stop that," Doree scolded. "If you start, we'll all be lost.

Hannah nodded. "For once, she's right."

Doree made a face at them.

The prelude music paused, then started again, signaling the procession to begin.

At Hannah's word, little Amber and Jenna, Guthrie's nieces—one blond, one brunette—wearing matching peach-colored dresses, started down the aisle scattering rose petals. Their younger brother, Hunter, paraded behind them, proudly holding up the white satin pillow to which two sets of wedding bands were tied.

When the three children reached the front, they went to sit beside their grandmother Martha and great-aunts Ida and Edith. Practical Hannah had decided children needed to be "anchored," not left to their own devices behind the two wedding couples.

Then Paloma, looking shy but very pretty in the peach gown originally meant for Spring, started down the aisle. From the groom's side of the church, Anita, Santos and *Tía* Rosita all beamed at her. Aunt Geneva and Matilde, sitting on the bride's side, dabbed their eyes and smiled encouragingly, too.

At the front of the church, Paloma took her place across from Pete Rasmussen, who'd flown up for the wedding. Exuberant Pete becoming Marco's closest friend ranked as another miracle on this day of wonders.

Lynda, Guthrie's sister, took her turn down the aisle. She stopped across from her husband, Bill. She and Bill had remarried in a private ceremony and were just back for a visit from the army base where they lived.

Always unpredictable Doree, the maid of honor,

paraded down the aisle as though it were all a play in which she was performing. She faced Brandon, the best man, Guthrie's older brother.

Then came the solution to the dilemma of this unusual wedding—with their father as the officiating minister, Bill Smith was to give the brides away. Now Bill Smith gave an arm to both the brides, his two newly discovered granddaughters, and led them to the altar.

Though Spring's joy on the occasion of her own and her sister's wedding filled her to overflowing, it didn't compare to the exultation of seeing her mother sitting beside her half brothers and half sister as they watched Bill walk Spring and Hannah down the aisle. Spring bit back tears.

At the front of the church, blond Guthrie and dark Marco, both handsome in black tuxes for the occasion, waited for their respective brides. Between them, the brides' father, Garner, waited to read the wedding service.

Garner began. "Dearly beloved, we are gathered here…"

Standing just a step away from Marco, Spring waited for the moment that would make her mother supremely happy.

Father asked the important question: "Who gives these brides to these grooms?"

Tall and silver-haired, Bill declared proudly, "I give these brides—though I've only known them a day." As his eyes filled with tears, he looked over at his newly found daughter. "Ethel, I know Connie is smiling down on us from heaven today. Your name tells me that Connie still loved me. You see, Ethel was my mother's name. Connie named you Ethel as a sign, so I'd know you were my own dear child.

"How I wish I could have held you in my arms as a baby and walked you down the aisle when you married Garner. But by the grace of God, I'm here today, and we'll make up for the time we've lost—if He gives me a few more years. Praise God, my children and I have a whole new family to love."

* * * * *

Dear Reader,

I hope you enjoyed the romance of Spring and Marco. Marco made the mistake many make. He substituted doing good for trusting in God. Marco had plans to help others, but he wanted to do it all by himself. Pride and guilt can be powerful but destructive motivations. He was fortunate to have a wise and caring mother!

I hope you were touched by the happy ending for Spring and Hannah, her sister, but especially the reunion of their mother with her natural father. What a beautiful day!

God bless you with His bountiful love and blessings!

Lyn Cote

Lyn Cote
P.O. Box 273
Hiawatha, IA 52233
http:/www.BooksbyLynCote.com